The Center of the Universe

Jakob Vedelsby

Translated from the Danish by
Nina Sokol

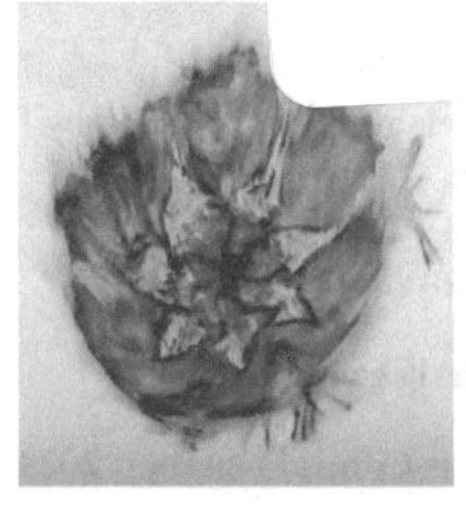

SPUYTEN DUYVIL

NEW YORK CITY

The citation in the chapter "A Last One at the Bonfire" derives from Claus Hempler's song "Op"

Special thanks to The Danish Arts Foundation for financial support towards the translation and publication of this book.

Danish Arts
Foundation

For Gitte, Frederikke and Josefine

All the gods, all the heavens,
all the hells, are within you.
Joseph Campbell

Limitless undying love which shines
around me like a million suns.
It calls me on and on across the universe.
Lennon-McCartney

They are approaching the island from the south. The invisible, dancing propeller is pulling the engine through the white cloud fog, through the strata of air as foot soles, thighs, backs, shoulders, arms, hands vibrate. The pilot puts out his cigarette stub, follows the coast and passes the lighthouse, winks at the woman by his side, thumbs up, her hand on his thigh, before them the bumpy patch of grass, a green pencil stroke in the landscape. He calls the control tower at the periphery of the airport but then the voice in the radio is drowned out by an ear-deafening sound, glass chips, bird's feathers fill the cabin, knives slash the face, she screams, reaches for him, the wind blowing through the wind shield, the distorted propeller. The engine banks, sparkling wave crests emit sparks, he tears at the steering wheel, brown-yellow steppes, scattered pine trees, a black shed. Silence when he finds her hand, and the light floats through them and disappears.

THE PULSE OF THE EARTH

The living room crept up on Bill with its low-hanging ceilings under which he could barely stand upright on his legs, the raw floor boards, impossible to clean, small, barred windows, and double glazed windows through which the wind hissed, crooked, lit candles standing in a stained brass candle holder, a yellowed map of the island, a landscape watercolor painting in a wooden frame, a mini stereo with a tape recorder, crackling loudspeakers on a shelf with encyclopedias, the rust-damaged, oval wood-burning stove standing on three legs, worn-down claret-colored carpets, a relatively recent upholstered sofa of charcoal gray woolen material. From his position at the stained dining table, which was decorated with rose hip branches from the desert, through the doorway, Bill had a view of a narrow kitchen leading to the entrance hall where there was access to the bathroom, the cork-tiled floor with a footpath, tabletops in laminated wood that were starting to disintegrate. He isolated the buzzing sound of the refrigerator, absorbed the brown floor-tiles of the bathroom, the walls of which were covered with sauna wood, the mustard-yellow bathroom sink, the toilet bowl with a Bakelite seat and the very bottom of the staircase that, from the kitchen, led steeply up to the first floor which was dark and which consisted of a room divided by a chimney. Bill blew out the candle, walked through the dining room and up the stairs with his head bent, hurled himself onto the creaking one-man bed positioned along the gable under the arching window hole, the softness of the duvet after many washes. The twilight melted his body, gradually the cadence of his heart subsided, clouds pursued one another and the first stars became visible.

Life in the Desert

It had now been a few days since Bill had stopped in front of the door to his apartment, registered the talisman, red-brown from reindeer blood and nailed firmly to the door, lifted his suitcase, took a deep breath as he opened the door, took one step forward and closed the door behind him. He arrived at the island early in the evening and had located the house which was bathed in the light of the setting sun.

Since then Bill had gone for walks in the golden, warm sand of the desert amongst heads of reptiles and black flints engraved in white lime areas, dried up lichen which turned to dust at the touch, blots of green and violet heather, sun-bleached bushes, butterflies here and there, the droppings of snakes, deer and rabbits, eagerly budding yellow flowers, almost obliterated footprints.

One day he walked all the way out to the lighthouse and was feeling particularly sorry for himself and the life fate had now handed to him. What does losing a parent do to a child? What process had it initiated in his brain, his nerve pathways, his emotional spectrum, his heart's ability to make the right choice? It had been a defining factor his whole life and even the most well-meaning therapist or romantic partner would never be able to alter that. Bill started running, leaving the desert behind him, the landscape of glowing eyes, the labyrinth of eternity, and managed to get back to the house. Overwhelmed by fatigue, full of longing for the empty rooms without memories, he crawled up the stairs and hurled himself onto the bed and registered the hectic sound of his parents' babbling voices as his mother and father spoke all at once, all the words they had showered him with from the moment he entered the world to the day they took off for the island to buy a summerhouse for the family. But now the words dissolved in the frozen wide expanses of the desert and he said to himself that it wasn't important what determined the course of his life now, whether it was random events or the genetic material he had brought with him, the codes his parents behavior had ingrained in him, people with whom he been intimate. The important thing was the moment which condensed that which came prior to it and that which awaited it in an undefined present. That was where he belonged, in that present here and now, now, now Bill floated in the universe, surrounded by twinkling stars and his eyes caught sight of a blue planet that came closer at a rapid pace as though he were sucked toward it, everything white and it was as though he was whirling through snow and caught sight of a humble log cabin. There was smoke coming out of the chimney and all at once he stood firmly planted on the ground, a man was stirring a pot on the stove which had been converted from an oil barrel. Bill stepped into the body, gasped for breath and turned toward a figure, Leonid, who was lying on a plank bed with his eyes shut.

A mouse had crawled up the staircase, through the insulation along the chimney or from the nest under the roof slope and was now sitting on the slightly torn sea grass blanket Bill had a tendency to trip over during his nightly visits to the bathroom, observed him with curiosity when he opened his eyes, motionless, even though he moved, stretched.

"Hello, friend," it said in a hoarse voice from the past, hesitating slightly. "Everything between darkness and light are insignificant nuances, and right now, Bill, you are standing in the middle of the darkness."

Bill was balancing on the edge of sleep but he registered the mouse gnawing at the tip of his pinky so that the blood colored the duvet dark-red like the sunset across the ocean when he met his lover and everything had been a blessed beginning. And when she left him and a time whirl grabbed hold of him, hurled him through the years, until it finally let go and he tumbled through darkness, planting his feet on the plains of nothingness and started walking.

A common strategy to overcome grief after having lost someone is to let one's sense of reality take over and cut off one's connection to the one who has disappeared using the explanation that if one dwells too much on it one risks getting into a depression. That seemed sound enough to Bill, only it required one make that emotional break which wasn't allowing itself to be carried into effect.

Even after the divorce everything struck him as unreal. At first he thought the condition was his mind's revenge over the uncompromising power of the work-devil which had the same features as obsession and was most probably what cost him his marriage, but there was no revenge, he had been depleted of content. Which was why he was standing at the kitchen table in a strange house waiting for the water to boil, opened the window, lit a cigarette, received the morning gift that was nicotine. He wasn't quite sure how long he was going to stay and where he was going to go afterwards. If there was an afterwards. He was going to visit Jonas, but there was something else calling to him. In dreams he had seen a woman standing alone in the desert in the night and hurling her heart-piercing sobs up toward the stars. Mie was the name of the house owner, he remembered now, could it be her? He had seen pictures of Mie on the internet in an interview about the life of a priest on a small island, the key in the flower pot with the lemon thyme to the right of the terrace door, a telephone number for questions.

Bill lit the three-legged wood-burning stove, breathless, toasted bread with goat cheese, Nescafe with cream, palm sugar, cigarettes. The sun moved, or the planet, the bright light through the window pane. He went out in the shrubby desert landscape, walked along the water to the lighthouse, the waves, yapping seals. On the way back the darkness permeated the membrane of his body, his toes, feet, ankle joints, shins, calf muscles, knees, knee tendons, upper thighs, lower thighs, buttocks, rectum, large intestine, small intestine, seminal vesicle, sperm duct, testicles, penis, bladder, ureter, stomach, ducts entering and exiting, prostate, appendix, pancreas, gall bladder, liver, kidneys, esophagus, heart, lungs, wind pipes, throat, mouth, face, nose, eyes, ears, brain, back of neck, shoulders, arms, hands, fingers, back, skin, blood, arteries, veins, tendons, muscles, bones, bone marrow, cells adapted to Schumann resonances. Then the light came, and star dust sailed through the sun-filled room.

THE PRIEST

The mouse had transformed into a woman with bare shoulders, a cold feline who slid under the duvet.

"Let's go on a journey," she whispered, whereupon they went down to the ocean, a row boat that had been hauled up on land, she crawled on board, he pushed the boat off the shore, rowed through the spin drift from the breakers, dark water, the slurping oars that vanished in water and resurfaced. He pulled off his shirt, muscles moving below his skin, she sat furthest back with her face toward him, her dress floating, silent, serious, the wind in her hair, until she was no longer there. He pulled in the oars, no coastline, the water heavy and calm, the mouse looked around with fearful eyes, shot up to the edge and jumped in.

*

Bill had just awoken after a long afternoon nap, balanced his way down the narrow steps of the staircase to the kitchen, when he remembered the agreement he had made with the priest, the lease had to be confirmed. He splashed some water in his face and ran to the vicarage where there were some children playing, but no one opened the door. So instead he went for a walk, through the town, and further, along the sandy gravel road toward the airport. There were two women standing in the middle of the road and talking to one another. Bill recognized the priest, her dog on a leash, she was speaking with a tall, dark-haired woman who looked at him with curiosity.

"Oh, that's right, we had an agreement, I'm sorry," said Mie who took a few steps in his direction.

"That's alright," he said.

"Do you like the house? Have you managed to settle in alright? It's so rundown."

"It's perfect," Bill said and hesitated. "But, tell me, the grocery store that's usually located on the periphery of town, has it changed location?"

Oddly enough he hadn't been able to find it and it carried a particularly fine brand of cognac, he recalled.

"I was told it closed several years ago, now there's only the supermarket," the dark-haired woman said.

Her voice was slightly hoarse, Bill couldn't take his eyes off of her lips, that moved, without it impacting her mimicry. Mie nodded in agreement.

"Oh, too bad, I liked the place," he said as he sensed a flash of happiness run through him, it had to do with Jonas, and with their childhood, it was the summer when they stayed on the island for two weeks, father, mother, his little brother and him.

"I actually worked there," said Mie. "And in the afternoons I minded the ice cream booth down on the harbor."

He immediately recognized her, the long, wavy, blond hair now settled across her shoulders, had been gathered into a thick braid back then.

"I think I remember you," she continued, "Didn't you come almost everyday to buy ice cream and candy?"

Bill nodded.

"You wore red sports glasses with curved sides that wound around your ears."

Mie laughed out loud. "That's right."

"Then we must have seen each other, too," the dark-haired woman said.

"Did you also come here as a child? What's your name?"

"Barbara. My father and I spent a few summers here. We would rent Mie's parents' annex, but I don't think I remember you."

"But I seem to recall … no, it's probably just my imagination," said Bill.

"It's a long time ago."

She kept silent, shuffled her feet a little.

"I should get going. It was nice meeting you, what's your name?"

"Bill."

"That's a name I can remember."

She locked him in her gaze, a flock of seagulls drifted across the sky.

"See you soon, Mic."

They watched Barbara as she disappeared down the path among the pine trees.

"We were girlfriends back then. She's changed a lot, however, and I don't know … she seems a little absent-minded. Suddenly she was just standing there in front of me. Strange how the past suddenly just washes over you."

They walked back toward town together, talked about the island in the old days. It must have just rained because the sand was dark and there were puddles on the gravel road.

"May I ask what you plan to do here? Is it work-related?"

"Actually, the opposite," said Bill. "I have been on a … a long and exhausting journey and am trying to regain my strength. And then I also want to visit my friend, Jonas."

"I wonder if I know him?"

"I doubt it. He is a patient at the new hospice and not particularly preoccupied with Christianity."

"Then I do know who he is. It's been a difficult process, from what I understand. I spoke with one of his sons rather recently. He is to be buried here on the island when his time comes."

"I wasn't aware of that. But he's always loved coming here. He and I have camped out here many times through the years."

"It's strange that you and I haven't run into each other before now."

She stopped in front of the gate with the white railing that surrounded the vicarage, let in the dog.

"Would you like to join me for a bite to eat? I have a dish in the oven, there'd be more than enough."

Bill hesitated.

"Come on. Look at it as part of the lease."

"I didn't know meals were included?"

"Then you haven't read the fine print."

He smiled and followed her through the garden and up the stairs. Inside, a flock of children came to greet them, she had four. The youngest was two and the oldest thirteen, there was no husband in sight, the children spoke all at once and he and Mie exchanged small talk in the warm kitchen. From where he was sitting in the kitchen he had a view of her workroom, the computer, the desk lamp resembled a boletus. Afterwards she wanted to show him the church, the two youngest ones were parked in front of the cartoons on TV, she assigned the two oldest to do the dishes which they reluctantly started on.

The church was located a few hundred meters from the vicarage and when they entered the cemetery he felt her hand in his and thought she wanted to show him some compassion because, naturally, he had to be sad that Jonas was fatally ill, and Bill considered telling her about the marks that the reindeer people had left in him, among other things, the knowledge that death is merely a transition to a new life which might make parting with Jonas slightly more manageable,

Above him the light green leaves of the oak tree

rustled and their footsteps made crushing sounds against all the small stones on the path. Mie inserted the key in the gaping key hole of the wooden door and he followed behind her through the rows of chairs. On the floor in front of the altar she turned around and pulled him close to her.

"Hold me," she whispered.

Her hand found its way to his crotch and he didn't try to stop it, now she was pulling her dress up, turned her back to him and bent over across the altar. She was burning hot when he penetrated her and he came fast, mumbled an apology, he couldn't remember the last time he had had sex.

"Brief, but good," she said and laughed. "We'll do it again, if you feel like it?"

She patted his cheek. Bill fumbled with buttoning his pants and then he broke into laughter and he embraced and kissed her.

"Are you an artist?" Mie asked, removing the drops from the stone floor with a handkerchief.

"Anthropologist. On temporary leave from university."

"Did you get tired of your work?"

"A lot has happened this past year. Five months out in the wilderness, and then I got divorced."

Bill sat down next to her on the cloth-covered elevation where the island's inhabitants would place their elbows when they went to Communion.

"If you ask me, our purpose here on earth is to recreate ourselves every moment and in that way give God the joy of experiencing the ultimate divine expression," she said in a serious voice.

"Perhaps that's what I am longing for, to recreate myself," he said, smiling.

"I just want to say that God wishes you to understand who you are and to make use of the power of God streaming through you, to unfold the plan you have for your life."

"I have no plan, not anymore."

She looked at him for a moment before she said, "Instead of drowning in emotions, you can make them concrete so they reveal themselves and in that way lose their grip on you."

The words sank through his skin like rain, like the most northerly sun after winter. Bill lay on the hard wooden surface and listened to the water trickling from the roof of the cottage. The ice melted faster in the blazing sun, and a brook emerged, meandering its way around rocks and bushes that had become visible under the snow. Spring was in full bloom, wild ducks and geese flew above them, the berry bushes created a green ground cover for the trees that were beginning to blossom, the northern Lapwing had arrived, embracing the landscape with its song.

Bill bade his farewell to Mie in front of the church. He floated to the supermarket like he was walking on air and bought minced meat, tomatoes, onions, red wine, cigarettes, oats, milk, sugar, sensing a quivering lightness in his body. His stomach rumbled, the night was young, the birds had awoken.

BUTTERFLIES

The summerhouse consisted of one storey, a living room, three claustrophobic rooms. Barbara slept on the couch in the living room even though there were no curtains and you could stand in the dark among the trees or with your face against the window pane and observe her. She hadn't seen a soul since she had left the ferry harbor, except for the bicycle delivery boy, a young man, handsome, who either yesterday or today had placed grocery bags from the supermarket beneath the roof of the shed as he, on the telephone, talked about his morning run, the sunrise, which had been particularly striking. Barbara had crisp bread with black currant marmalade, black coffee.

She had rented out her apartment and like some Buddha figure she had embarked on the unknown only to sit all alone under the holy fig tree and wait for the light, as a friend of hers tauntingly exclaimed when she realized that any direct contact they had had before would from now on be terminated.

"Or Moses who climbed the mountain," Barbara said as she laughed, just to say something. She was unable to give a more thorough explanation.

Later a text message appeared from her friend: Barbara could contact her when she had returned to this planet.

A mosquito buzzed across her face looking for a place to land. The living room was drenched in sunlight, the mosquito was now silent, had found shelter in a crack in the wood, or perhaps on top of one of the picture frames, no, it was sitting on her hand that was resting on the sofa table. She let the mosquito bore its proboscis into her vein, watched as the little creature swelled and took on a reddish hue. By the time the mosquito finally tore itself away it could barely keep itself afloat in the air, ascending higher and finding a resting place on the rosette below the ceiling. At that very moment a scream from two throats hammered inside the interior of her skull and white fog pulsated from the walls, forced its way through the room and dissolved everything it encountered. She got up, her feet stuck to the floor, each step required that she put her foot forth and set it back down. She opened the terrace door, her thoughts floating amongst the clouds, a wound that couldn't heal, he turned toward her, she wanted to say that he mustn't leave her in a world to which she didn't belong without him, without the children they never had, what was to become of them?

Rainbow-colored soap bubbles in the sun across the meadow when they walked toward the sea shore with their picnic basket, unpacked it, a white sheet on the grass, plates, glasses, strawberry juice, rye bread, sausages, cucumber slices, cookies for dessert, mother's lips moving, do you want anymore to eat, are you thirsty, grandma's voice, do you want another cookie, father's lips with the cigarette, he clears his throat, points toward two white butterflies hovering above the lake. The voices existed, the ones she had taken over from them, and those that existed beforehand, eternity, bodies reduced to dust underneath a blanket of daisies, She slid down on her back, followed the seagull circling above her where everything existed, the hand that stroked her hair. She caught her mother's gaze, crawled into it, into the forest, and up into the tallest tree, up among the clouds and down the dusty gravel road that meandered through the landscape.

FAREWELL

Barbara thought that you were in the right relationship if it began as a dream that transformed itself into a nightmare, when old traumas surfaced so they could be healed but she discovered a love relationship wasn't necessarily able to contain the accompanying baggage and they had certainly listened attentively if there were things they were unable to handle themselves. Add to that their shared experiences which they didn't know how to overcome, either. Painful treatments against childlessness, the joyful pregnancy, the miscarriage, the tiny, dead corpse in the shiny steel basin late one night. They never talked about the boy in the steel basin, as the years passed through them like waves, and they approached the point when it was time to part ways that planted a terrifying seed that night and slowly took shape in them both.

*

Almost a year had passed since that night, Barbara lay in bed sensing the warm summer breeze through the crack in the balcony door, observed her husband's lips were moving. It wasn't anything he had made up, he had extracted it from books in which he was always buried when they could have been holding each other, kissed, made love, he read extracts out loud to her, she listened, and longed for who they were.

"I am to venture out into the world to find my way home," he said and she understood that he had consulted a therapist, a ready-to-deliver self-delusion.

She thought about the time when they first met in the university cafeteria and struck up a conversation at the buffet. It was probably his blond curls that caught her attention, or his finely shaped nose, or the fact they made each other laugh. He cleared the dirty dishes and they walked through town, he invited her to a restaurant and afterwards they went to a bar, went home to her dormitory and talked for the rest of the night about the things they dreamt about. The next morning they kissed and when he biked home she felt more sensitive, determined, and ready than ever before. It wasn't long before she didn't do anything without first consulting him.

"I have read about a monk who provides an all-embracing piece of advice to each individual who seeks him out," he continued.

"And what would he say to you?"

"Something that will pull me out of the lethargic state I'm in."

He turned off the light, they lay in silence on their backs and stared at the ceiling, her hand caressed the bristly hair on his chest, moved further down across his stomach, and further still between his thighs. He sat up, said he was afraid of not leaving something of significance, as if he had never been here. He sat at the edge of the bed, his leg trembling, as though he couldn't decide whether to stay or go, she put her arms around him, the soft tuft on the back of his neck against her lips.

"It is painful to long for something you're unable to carry out," he said and got up. "The pressure inside is mounting and I will never be able to pave the way into that which is me. I must be inside there somewhere."

She pulled him back down to the bed.

"Would you please be so kind as to return to reality so we can talk about this as adults?"

"I thought together with you I'd be able to dissolve all the resistance I have inside me," he whispered.

She felt like screaming or, at the very least, crying,

and at that very moment she couldn't remember what it was that had bound them to one another for all those years. She took a deep breath.

"Just because you believed in something for a long time doesn't mean you have to believe in it forever," she said calmly, and heard her father say the same words in a triumphant tone as he pointed straight in front of him, before he set off running for the butterfly sailing obliviously through the low desert hills.

He shook his head and turned away and she thought he was about to dissolve in all his self-absorption, an aimless search for a clarification of something that couldn't be clarified but which had to be lived through, the child they had lost, the phases of life, that's how everybody was put together, there were ups and downs, momentary confusion on the way to great insights which he either couldn't or wouldn't acknowledge. A psychologist could help, maybe a psychiatrist, taking medicine for a period of time until he settled down and was better able to get an overview of the situation, but something more was needed. No less than a surging, all encompassing life crisis, something demanding self exploration for months or even years at a time.

"I must delve deeper within myself." He looked at her intensely. "And I have found a way."

She thought of the outline of the horizon, the wind, the waves, a monk in a monastery at the top of a hill. His eyes were shiny and she felt her sense of helplessness gradually transforming into one of contempt.

"I've bought a one-way ticket." He put his arms around her. "You'll be fine. Everything will fall perfectly into place."

"I don't think it's possible to figure your whole life out in that way and I'm pretty certain the process of finding yourself won't go any faster in a monastery than being with me. You'll come to regret what you're about to do."

She could no longer control her voice and freed herself from his embrace and went out to the bathroom, locked the door, turned on the shower,and pounded her fists against her thighs.

"I don't know why I'm here," he said from the hallway, to himself, to her.

"Shut up you heartless narcissist," she whispered.

"And I continue to wander in hopes of catching some of those insights that are whirling around me.

There is something beyond me that I want to reach for, something that can ignite a spark within me ”

It became quiet in the hallway. Now Barbara heard his footsteps in the entrance hall, held back her tears and ran after him.

Real's Wood White

The evening Barbara's husband left her she didn't dare close her eyes, she just lay staring into space, towns and landscapes grew from the shadows on the wall. Now a sound got her heart pounding, a movement across the floor of the summerhouse, it was hammering, her body was swaying back and forth, branches scraped against the window section as tall as a man and now the sky was illuminated by flashes of light, the sound of an explosion made the window sills shake, rolling through her like flashes of memories at the moment of death.

She wasn't used to being alone and certainly not in an unfamiliar house far away from other houses, from the city, surrounded by creaking trees, the ocean that stretched forth its arms of waves, pulling her down to the dead fishermen, their crushed boats and gurgling screams that echoed in submerged walls. Butterflies floated between one another at the bottom of the ocean and her father came walking along with a fishing net, swung it without catching anything, her mother standing there with her arms crossed laughing at him, and now a little girl appeared behind the big man and it was she herself.

*

When Barbara, at age ten, asked her father why they'd gotten divorced he said her mother had no longer been able to live with him. They were on vacation together alone on the island, on the butterfly summer vacation trip, as he called it, which had first and foremost to do with a particularly rare species that hadn't been spotted for many years.

"But it's here in the desert somewhere, I can feel it. Broken white, almost transparent, like the tulle of a wedding dress, its wingspan over 32 and sometimes all the way up to 43 millimeters, its name: Real's Wood White," he said.

Barbara had heard it before, it was practically indistinguishable from the Wood White. They walked through the desert in the direction of the island's northern side, the wet sand stuck to their shoes, after the rain the butterflies appeared in great numbers.

"There!" her father shouted, his eyes wide open and, his teeth bared, he swung the net.

The butterfly looked for an opening to freedom . He nudged it down into the poison glass that contained sawdust on its bottom, then plaster and a layer of cotton with some drops of acetic ether.

"For a moment I thought it was a Green Underside Blue but it's just a common Blue. Not exactly rare, but decent swapping material, and a good way to start the day," he said.

Barbara let her hand disappear into his and he practically pulled her along with him through the sand until he let go and pointed at something. Two white butterflies sat perched each on their own yellow flower, sipping nectar, and Barbara caught herself wishing they would fly away so as to avoid the fate her father had in store for them. Death in the marmalade jar followed by a day and a half in the softening box with moist paper on the bottom until the stiffness of death started to wear off. Whereupon he would lace them on the the stretching board, unfold the wings into the right position and fasten them with thin needles.

Their forelegs and antennae would get smoothed out, then they would have to dry for a month whereupon he would remove the needles and fasten them to the display board.

The two white butterflies sensed the huge shadow and flew away the very moment he swung the net, thereby avoiding the wooden box with the glass lid stored in the protective darkness of a closet. Six boxes with butterflies in straight rows. Two rows containing ten each.

"What does that come to?" he asked and didn't wait for her response: "200 in each box, that makes 1200 all in all. Plus all the extra, and minus the holes."

The seventh box was for particularly rare species. The sheet was almost completely empty, she counted eight in all. That was where the Wood White would end if he managed to catch it.

"*When* I catch it," he said with confidence.

She saw him sitting alone at the work table in the room dedicated to butterflies, he turned round in his chair and placed his hand on her shoulder. It smelled of vinegar. Her mother had gone on vacation somewhere with her sister. Long afterward Barbara was told she had gotten a job in the opposite side of the country and the next thing she was told was that they had gotten a divorce.

Barbara didn't understand why her mother couldn't

live together with her father. She was under the impression that mother would die if they stayed together, and since she herself identified mostly with her father she began to think she perhaps was also a person with whom one couldn't live together, a person who was dangerous to be around. Later she had the feeling she herself took up too much space and when her husband was sad she would blame herself, concluding that it had to be because she was somehow preventing him from living his life to the fullest. On their second date they sauntered through the city, but what did they in fact talk about? She remembered seeing him stopping and pointing at the front door.

"This is where I live, wanna come up and have a beer?"

"Do you have wine?"

"Of course I have wine."

He put the key into the lock, held the door for her and that was that.

Familiar Faces

Barbara pulled the knitted sweater over her head, threw a scarf around her neck and slammed the door shut to the summerhouse.

She needed to move her body and walked along the trail that went through the forest in the direction of the desert, the forest, which she knew so well, was the same and yet changed. Trees disappeared and others had taken their place through the years. The scent hadn't changed, birds sang just as always and the trail was located in the same place it had always been. There was no doubt in Barbara's mind who it was that came walking in her direction with a dog. There in the desert, decades ago, Mie had also walked her dog, which was, like now, a mixed breed with golden fur. There was something familiar about the tall, slightly gray-haired man who a little while later stepped out of nowhere and stopped in front of them. Perhaps she had seen him on TV or seen his picture in the newspaper where he'd been interviewed about whatever it was he did or an experience he'd had. Everybody ended up in the media someway or other. As soon as she saw him she immediately thought he was one of those men who wanted to, but who couldn't conceal the fact that he cultivated his feelings like a bonsai, looking after and caring for his inner universe, finding himself in an utter state of confusion as a result while at the same time maintaining a facade of masculine self-confidence. In that way he reminded her a little of her ex-husband although they physically had very little in common. The man she had lived together with was shorter and his shoulders more narrow, his skin as soft as a baby's and he had had slender office fingers, while the man standing across from her showed signs of having consumed his fair share of whiskey, cigarettes, white bread and had forgotten all about salads.

He wasn't classically handsome, but then again. She sensed his scrutinizing gaze when she left them which confused her and she didn't understand why. In the shelter of the pine trees she turned and looked at the figures in the desert landscape, a trembling sensation in her stomach moved down through her legs and along the backside of her body and stung like needles on the back of her neck and head. She disengaged herself from the party and walked toward the water until she reached that small piece of the island that was hers, overgrown after all these years, remained standing for a little in the clearing of the property among the trees before continuing in the direction of town and entering the supermarket. A young man with a ponytail was putting items in place, the bicycle delivery boy, he was staring. Could you tell by looking at her she was scared of waking up from the nightmare because reality was more frightening or was he attracted to her because she was a woman, because strangers were a rare sight to see on the island outside of peak season which was just about to begin? She turned toward him and wanted to say something, a customer-friendly smile spread on his face, but at that very moment a man entered the shop so Barbara continued filling her basket with items, paid the cashier lady, walked at a rapid pace back to the house, collapsed in the armchair and observed the skin between her thumb and index finger on her right hand which was moving up and down.

*

Barbara told herself that life consisted of endless paradoxes. You had to be prepared to surrender whatever explanatory models you had been referencing until now and open yourself to new ones. But why couldn't her ex-husband love that which life had given him? She passed the rocky stretch of beach and picked up the pace, foam from the waves floating around her. She shook her body. He was cynical when he said that he, like all other humans, longed for unconditional love because that was where we came from and through which we were born.

Now she was alone and no matter how much energy her girlfriends invested trying to imagine her emotional state they would never be able to fully fathom the torment which life was now subjecting her to. If they tried to project themselves on her, nothing but the same stereotypical version would result, and the same would obviously be true the other way around. It was the case when she lost her child and again when she was abandoned.

Which was why Barbara never told anyone that during the days subsequent to his departure she was unable to conjure anything other than meaningless questions: When would he return, what would it take to get him back, what did she have to do, how could he do without her, what should she say to him, what would others have done in her place, should she call him or write what it was doing to her or him, what did she have to say or do to get him back?

Sometimes she found herself crying, automatically, practically coughing. She was never going to let him know that her longing was like a hunger that couldn't be satisfied, an abysmal hole that continued to grow. Time felt like it was on fast forward, as though it had continued on ahead and every present moment was a flash of memory of something that had taken place long ago. One day she sought the place where he, after his return from that ridiculous journey of self-discovery, was living with his new girlfriend, darkness had settled in as she drove through the neighborhood with its identical detached houses, hedges trimmed yet again to knee height, thin cuttings of apple and plum from the plant nursery, the clouds pulled in from the east, dew settled as droplets on the windshield, warm lights from the eyes of the windows. Barbara stopped in front of the house, turned off the engine. In the corner of the yard facing the road there was a birch tree as tall as a man, which in another ten to fifteen years would be substantial enough for their kids to be able to hide in the branches of the tree top, sway back and forth in the wind, observe stars, keep an eye on what was going on in the road and the surrounding yards.

The range of light from the kitchen window revealed red and black currant bushes, a rhubarb bed, he took some plates and glasses from the cabinet, sat at the dining table and a likewise dark haired woman walked in and sat down.

"I hate you," Barbara whispered and saw the words roll across the not yet fused grass turf and through the kitchen window.

He turned, his gaze through the darkness blinded her and she started the car and drove away. Her tears remained stuck behind a practically obliterated face in the palms of her hands, her will power directed her movement through darkness blacker than death. Suddenly she started laughing loudly when she realized it was all definitively over. The son they had lost and the chaos in which they had gone astray had multiplied itself within them, and the laughter transformed to sobs and back to laughter, she turned off at the highway and increased the speed to match the music coming from the stereo, sensing how she pulled off the straitjacket he had already tossed far away and at that very moment a part of her melted in the glowing light from oncoming traffic while another part of her tumbled toward a dark center form which she had to disengage from so that she could sprout anew, who lay like a pile of garbage at the edge of a field with wavy grass, an ocean of red and yellow flowers.

Above the field there floated a cloud of white butterflies.

There was no wind, the ocean as smooth as a mirror. Bill shook water from his hair and wrapped himself in a towel. Two yellow kayaks were moving along the coast, he sat on the sand and observed when one of them put down a paddle to rest and waved. Bill didn't recognize him, waved back, they took off at rapid speed. It had been many years since Bill had gone kayaking, the last time had been during their last visit to the island. Before Jonas got sick.

Jonas and he grew up in the same town. Bill slept on a mattress on the floor in his room the first few weeks after the accident before he was put up with a foster family. As adults they would go almost every summer, and always during the same week, on a camping trip and stayed at the camp site in the north part of the island not far from the harbor. Last time they talked about what kind of a building being put up on the plateau on the hill above the site. It was now completed, and Bill made his way up the street that smelled of new asphalt, hesitated in front of the glass door before entering the air-conditioned reception area and was given a room number.

The contours of Jonas's even teeth appeared through the tight skin surrounding his mouth. He slumbered, was practically unrecognizable as if a foreign creature moved into his body and the sense of guilt struck Bill for not having been there for him for the last many months. Jonas opened one eye halfway when he sat on the chair by the bed rail.

"Is that you again?" he asked as though they had just seen each other a moment before.

The week before Bill had taken on this expedition they had dinner together and Jonas had been in good shape.

"Did you come all the way over here just to visit me?"

"We're in week 25," said Bill, giving him a light tap on the shoulder.

"How could I forgot? Help me up, will you?"

Bill stuck his arm underneath his and supported him over to the window. They stood for a moment looking at the camp site and the ocean.

"I'm happy I managed to get a spot here."

Bill nodded.

"I've always looked forward to week 25 like a little kid," Jonas continued.

"Me too."

At that very same moment Jonas's body heaved forward and he grabbed hold of his stomach, his face as white as the walls.

"I have to get back to bed," he moaned, crawling back under the covers and pulling the cord for the nurse.

"How did your journey go?" he asked in a whisper, avoiding Bill's glance.

Bill hadn't told him what exactly he had gone out to investigate. It somehow seemed wrong to entertain Jonas alongside tribal people's relationship and death. Instead, he pulled up his shirt and displayed five parallel scars, still red at the edges, stretching from his right collar bone and running down across his chest and ending at his left hip.

"That's from the bear I wrote about."

Bill put his hand in his pocket, pulled out a bear's claw and handed it to Jonas.

"All the way from the wilderness to you."

A moist film glazed over Jonas' eyes.

"Give me the story," he said as he exhaled.

"Are you sure?"

"If not now, when? I've been waiting for it for a long

time. But first tell me a little bit about the area you visited."

Bill described the endless wilderness that was just as frightening and just as wonderful as he remembered it from his travels during his student days and that oscillated between a feeling of unstoppable happiness, finding himself in a virginal winter painting, and an endless fear of wild nature's relentless will to destroy all living things. This time he had traveled the transitional zone between a humongous primal forest with pine, larch, birch and willow trees and the barren ice desert that you can fly across for hours on end without registering any life. The vegetation consisted chiefly of low, wispy bushes and everything was deeply frozen.

Bill had gotten to his feet and stood by the window and looked out across the ocean when Jonas cleared his throat with a raspy wheeze from his bronchi. Bill turned around and caught a transparent gaze, sat down on the chair by the bed rail and continued:

"At the end of winter, in February, Leonid, my guide and interpreter, and I lived with the reindeer people for three months and were in a sleigh on our way back to the town from where I was to fly home when we hit a snow storm. By way of incredible luck, we had just arrived at one of those hunting lodges with hundreds of kilometers between them.

When the storm finally moved on, our reindeer had managed to get away and our supplies had run out.

Jonas's eyes sunk into their sockets and his breathing became raspy. Bill observed him for a moment. He reminded him a great deal of Leonid who, after several weeks of not getting any food, was completely depleted and lay down most of the time. Leonid managed to remain optimistic for a long time and Bill watched as he stomped on the perma frost and paced around the lodge to get some life back in his muscles, stopped in his tracks to straighten the tattered plastic bags that comprised a window. A few pots and pans hung from wires from the ceiling beams and a few plates were standing on a shelf. Their backpacks were leaned up against the wall between beds. Bill could just manage to stand up straight in the lodge which consisted of untreated logs and was scantily insulated with moss. At floor level the temperature was permanently minus 20 and reached 40 below in the morning hours when the fire had gone out. For that reason, they would cut wood chips and dry them in the oven every night so they were ready to be lit first thing in the morning, whereupon the men would remain in their sleeping bags until the lodge had warmed.

"I can imagine what it must feel like to starve," Jonas immediately said from the depths of the bed. He was still listening.

"Then try to imagine hunger and extreme cold in combination with one another. But it was also gorgeous there."

The moment had etched itself in his conscience. In the morning, when the faint sun appeared through the mist he pulled on his fur outfit and took the rifle down from the wall. The air cut like shards of glass in his lungs and moisture on his skin surrounding his eyes turned to ice and made a crackling sound when he blinked. In a distance which Bill was unable to estimate, mountain chains hung like heavy jewels from the clouds.

"I thought of you many times when I was lying in that lodge and starving, about our trips together and I decided if I, contrary to all expectations, returned alive, I would come over to the island and stay for a little while."

"Like me," Jonas said, attempting a smile. "But what about the bear? That was what you were to tell me out," he said in a hoarse voice.

Bill nodded slowly as he considered where he should start.

"I don't remember how long we'd been in the lodge the first time I noticed paw prints. It was a lone male who was roaming about and Leonid said killing that bear would be practically impossible. The bear's fur was like an armor of ice in the winter and the only way you can be sure of killing it is by hitting it with a bullet either through its mouth or its arm pit."

Jonas' closed eyes trembled.

"Go on," he whispered.

"There were only a few hours left til sundown and my actions were being directed by forces beyond my control. I stopped in my tracks and looked out across the frozen landscape, no wind, no animals, just the all encompassing silence, and yet still I felt as though someone was keeping an eye on me."

"Was it the bear or your imagination?"

"I don't know," Bill said slowly.

The snow underneath the skis crackled and his

breath emitted fogs of steam into the air. His legs carried him in the direction of the river and when he passed the thicket with the low shrubbery he caught sight of a bonfire to the east and stopped abruptly in his tracks. It was hardly a hunter, but then it would have to be the spirits playing tricks on him. Staring eyes hit him from all directions when he forced his skis further across the snow, picked up the speed and moved away from the imaginary bonfire, crossed the frozen river and passed a big cohesive forest area.

Jonas stirred restlessly.

"Does it hurt?" Bill asked.

He nodded with pain.

"Could you pull the cord? Maybe I didn't pull it hard enough."

Jonas turned on his side so that he was facing Bill.

"Go on. What happened then?"

Bill did what he had learned from the native hunters, crawled into one of the few semi-tall trees and scanned the area for animal tracks in the snow. But there were none to be seen. When he was once again standing on firm ground a sense of exhaustion moved through his body without warning like liquid lead and he fell to his knees.

"It felt as though everything around grew foggy, all my energy sucked out of my body and I fell forward. When I, with tremendous effort, managed to pull my face out of the snow I saw something red in all the whiteness and started digging. A plant emerged and a handful of stone-hard berries were growing on its branches."

Jonas's body jerked.

"Were they edible?"

"I risked it, kept them in my mouth for a long time before swallowing and continued until there weren't any left. And then suddenly my arms and legs woke up and I was able to see more clearly."

Jonas nodded imperceptibly and Bill described how he continued north from there, along the river, and at one point he registered a sound that resembled the grunt of an animal, stopped and listened. The sound came again, louder than before, and something rummaged behind a growth of willow bushes a ways ahead in the distance. He was able to see a shadow moving and quietly pushed his skis off his feet and crawled a few meters ahead on all fours. With blood pounding through his ears, he placed the rifle against his cheek and emptied the magazine in direction of the shadow. The shots sounded like firecrackers he and his little brother threw on the cement floor in the basement below the house on New Year's Eve. Bill couldn't tell whether he had managed to hit anything and crawled on his stomach toward the shrubbery. He didn't have any more cartridges, and if it was the bear and it had only been injured it would kill him right there on the spot. He took the last steps round the bushes. There were blood stains in the snow and footprints of a bear that had escaped.

It was growing increasingly dark when Bill limped back through the snow in his own footprints. At long last, the lodge appeared and he opened the door and collapsed. The effect of the berries from the night before had worn off by morning and when he swung his legs over the edge of the plank bed he only felt like one thing, and that was to lie down and go back to sleep.

The sun was balancing on the horizon line when he lit the fire under the pot filled with the melted snow and drank a couple of mug fulls, threw a few more logs in the oven. The fire grew bigger and he pulled the stool over and let his gaze disappear into the flames as his body absorbed the heat. There was no escaping having to fell a couple of trees and chopping them for wood this morning, either, and from a layer of his consciousness still functioning he performed the task, dragging larch logs behind him, when he discovered bear tracks close to the lodge. Leonid was still lying in his sleeping bag, the only thing protruding from it was his worn, pale face.

Bill stood at the door and listened but there was nothing to hear but the wind that cast sharply pointed ice crystals against its wood work. He heard some rummaging behind him. Leonid sat up and was putting on his boots, got up on his feet, grabbed his worn rifle and staggered out and bent down over the tracks that cut through the layers of ice and snow all the way down to the surface of the ground. Leonid closed his eyes, his nostrils moved.

"When did the bear return?" Jonas asked with renewed energy in his voice.

"The following morning. It attacked us and I shot and killed it."

Jonas gave him a stern look, waved the bear claw in the air.

"I can handle hearing about it."

Bill described how he and Leonid registered a deep, growling sound. A good distance down the slope a dark animal stood on its hind legs, the bear had discovered them long ago, and now it was hurling itself forward running on all fours up to the lodge. Leonid reacted too late to manage to pull the trigger of his rifle. Bill instinctively took a few steps back and watched as the big animal set off and landed on one of Leonid's legs. It broke like a match and when he started screaming, the bear grabbed hold of him and flung him several meters away. He remained lying on the ground motionless, silent. Bill's glance wandered between the weapon that lay in the snow where Leonid had dropped it and the bear that was turning in his direction. He hurled himself forward and managed to grab hold of the rifle and pulled the trigger but the old piece of junk from some war or other got jammed. The bear started to growl, towered before him and he felt a stinging pain as it scratched its claws down across his chest.

He fell on his back and continued to pull and tear at the rifle and suddenly it worked and he fired at the bear's head. He must have hit its mouth because the animal jerked and fell forward, landing heavily in the snow.

Jonas was now sitting halfway up in bed and looking expectantly at Bill.

"The next thing I remember is that I was lying next to the bear and looking up at the sky transforming into a roaring ocean with red, yellow and blue waves rushing over me. I held the rifle close to my body, the front of my outfit had been torn open and I felt a sharp pain in my chest. When I tried to sit up the pain spread to one of my shoulders and I started throwing up."

"What about your guide, Leonid?"

"I crawled over to him. One of his legs lay in a completely wrong position but he still had a pulse. For a little man he weighed quite a bit in his outfit and I dragged him through the snow and into the lodge as blood ran from my pants and down my boots. I lay Leonid on the bed and removed his outfit and without knowing what I was doing I managed to push his broken bone more or less back into place and wrapped a bandage tightly around his leg. Whereupon I fired up the oven and it wasn't until the heat had spread throughout the lodge I began to shake all over.

I melted a potful of snow and rinsed the bruises with water. Then I heated up the hunting knife and burnt the flesh in the places from which blood was oozing. The strange thing was I couldn't feel anything. But that changed completely once I started getting back to myself later that day."

"It's a miracle you're even sitting here," said Jonas, letting his head sink back on the pillow. "And boy am I happy you are."

"It's something close to a miracle, yes. Would you like more juice?"

Bill was busy skinning the bear, he cut off chunks of the animal's meat and tied it to a piece of wood and put wolf traps in the snow. Then he filled yet another pot with snow and dumped the meat and fat into it and brought it all to a boil. The steam from the soup pot surrounded him and drifted up toward the ceiling.

"Thanks, just give me a drop."

Bill observed Jonas' trembling hand that guided the straw between his lips. Then he took the bear claw and scrutinized it.

"It's strange to think you actually cut it off the bear yourself," he said.

"I only took one of them and I took it for you. The shamans I met on the journey were wearing bear claws around their necks because they empower you and at the same time protect you."

Jonas looked up and caught Bill's gaze.

"Do they also give protection against death?"

"Maybe. It could very well be possible, couldn't it?"

Jonas remained silent for a little while before saying, "How would you prefer to die, Bill?"

"I'd like for it to be fast. Getting a blow from a bear, maybe. Freezing to death isn't supposed to be so bad, either. You just fall asleep."

Jonas nodded.

"I'd choose one of those options, too."

He lifted his arm a couple of centimeters above the duvet and pointed toward the window.

"I've considered jumping out but I'm afraid I wouldn't die from it."

He coughed or laughed, and Bill smiled faintly.

"But tell me what happened to your interpreter. Did he make it?"

"Fortunately. Leonid's bones grew back together more or less adequately but he was still limping and had cut himself a cane when the light and heat returned and we started hiking along the river back to civilization."

"How long did it take you?"

"A few weeks, I think. The worst thing were the mosquitoes. There were millions of them and they were blood-thirsty as hell." Bill turned his face toward Jonas.

"I tried calling you when we finally reached the city but the mobile network was down."

"What did you want?"

"To hear if you were alright."

"Well, I wasn't, and look at me now," said Jonas, attempting a smile. "I've reached the final chapter, as they say."

"That's not necessarily true. I brought some cognac, by the way."

"Of course you did."

"I'll get us some cups," said Bill and went out into the hallway.

He took some plastic cups from the steel table with tableware and got out the bottle.

"Imagine, our old general store has shut down and all they had was cheap cognac in the supermarket," Bill said apologetically.

"That's okay. My taste buds are pretty useless these days anyway."

Jonas's gaze turned toward the ceiling. Bill took his hand and carefully squeezed it, noticed the silence even though the ocean lay a few meters away.

"I'm sorry for sitting here blabbering away about myself. It's really so unimportant," said Bill.

"What do you mean?"

"You're lying here. That's what's important."

"It won't be long before I'm gone."

Bill's brain came to a standstill. There was so much he wanted to say but the sentences seemed to get stuck inside him.

"Do you remember we always used to play badminton in the street?" Jonas continued.

"Yeah, my guess is you won each time."

"For the most part, but we were pretty even."

"We'd certainly play for hours on end and your mom would bring us juice so we wouldn't get dehydrated."

"Why do you think I keep thinking about it?"

"I don't know. I guess we had fun."

"That we always have had."

"More cognac?"

He nodded. They sat for a moment looking at each other until a clucking sound came bubbling out of Jonas's mouth.

"This is kind of crazy, I can't make heads or tails of it, but I guess there's nothing to understand, is there?" he asked.

Bill shook his head and once again they sat for a long time without saying anything. Bill decided that he would after all tell Jonas about the reindeer people's relationship with death but at that very moment the door opened and a nurse entered, delivered a cup containing pills and disappeared again. Jonas rinsed them down with some cognac and a short moment later he was floating somewhere between the worlds and nodded imperceptibly when Bill whispered in his ear that he would soon return.

Before he left, Bill opened the window slightly so the air and sounds from the ocean could reach his friend, stopped and looked at him buried in the white duvet, collected the bear claw from the floor and placed it on the table cart. His longing for deep tranquility of the wilderness hit him after the moments of complete intimacy, stored in the magical borderland where new

realities made themselves known like when the raven
left a lump of droppings and kernels that sank down
into the soil and became trees and bushes and created a
world without being aware of it.

*

The following day after lunch Bill stood once again
before the young woman at reception. He said he knew
the way.

"I'll call the nurse," she responded.

"Jonas and I are childhood friends."

She nodded and turned back toward the screen.
Perhaps he was sleeping? Time passed. She pointed to
the sofa arrangement in front of the window wall facing
the green trimmed lawn stretching down across the
hill and toward the sea.

"Help yourself to a cup of coffee and enjoy the view."

Bill walked over to the window. Perhaps he was taking
a bath or receiving a visit from his physiotherapist? The
camp site resembled itself. How many times hadn't they
stayed the night there in each their own little tent and
made twist bread, grilled sausages and drunk beer? It
was down there Jonas, joyful and anxious about the

future, announced he was going to be a father for the first time.

The sound of squeaking rubber soles, and Bill turned toward the white-clad woman who stopped in front of him.

"Your friend died a short while ago. It went very fast in the end."

"That can't be true. I don't think we're talking about the same person," he said in a voice that echoed against the cement surfaces.

"I'm very sorry, but he did in fact die quite suddenly due to internal bleeding. It's something we seldom see but we do see it happen every so often to some patients receiving the particular pain-killers Jonas was receiving."

A sense of unrest spread through Bill's body.

"The family is in there now," she continued.

"The children?"

"Yes, his sons."

Bill nodded. He wanted to go in and see Jonas but didn't know his sons so well, sensed the nurse's hand on his shoulder. He looked up, nodded and walked toward the exit.

"Do you want me to tell them you were here?"she asked and he shook his head.

Behind Bill in the reflection of the glass door another figure appeared. He saw that it was Jonas and felt a hand under his arm. It was just as he had said, Jonas wasn't dead, they had confused him with someone else. The nurse's eyes must have popped as Jonas passed right by her. Bill put his arm around his shoulder and together they walked down the asphalt road, passed the camp site and reached the sea.

They removed their shoes and walked a little at the water's edge before Jonas moved all at once up above the beach. When he reached the top of the dune he turned and waved and at that very same moment the wind erased all his traces in the sand.

Bill continued along the beach until he took off his clothes, walked into the waves and started to swim along the coast. To be alive. He did the crawl until he lost his breath, took a break at the surface, pounded the water to foam. To be dead. A sparkling burst of energy rushed through the universe toward a new existence. He trudged up to the beach and let his body dry in the wind, put on his clothes and went back to the summerhouse.

Bill collapsed into a chair on the terrace with coffee and cigarettes and once again felt his longing for wilderness, his castles in the air, a mystery of boundless dimensions of which he only sensed an iota and would never be able to fully perceive. He was a mere fragment among millions of others, but it offered a sense of connection with totality. His eyes closed, he heard a man clear his throat from a distance of twenty years and all at once his thesis supervisor, the internationally acclaimed professor of the Institute, appeared and said in a tired voice that all talk of shamans and spirits were a waste of time in a world that clamored for rationality and science.

He sat at his polished mahogany desk behind a colossal computer screen. Now he pushed the desk chair a little out, straightened up, something in him creaked.

"Let's get the fundamentals in place," he continued, keeping his hand suspended in the air. "When the indigenous people talk about spirits it's a metaphor for something else, because spirits don't exist, which all the rest of us are perfectly well aware of. The truth is they worship their own society, they just aren't aware of it."

The professor's gaze kept lingering on the book case that filled the wall as though he were searching for a specific work that could emphasize his point. Bill didn't have to check to know the books had been painstakingly set in alphabetical order. Then the professor turned toward him but Bill beat him to the punch:

"Isn't that equivalent to dismissing millennia of experiences as pure fantasy?"

The professor crossed his arms, smiled roguishly as he always did during his classes, and you never knew whether his response would be that of approval or the opposite.

"No, it's the same as saying supernatural forces don't exist but science exists."

"As I see it, there's talk of rich universes from which we at the very least ought to allow ourselves to retrieve inspiration from," said Bill and stood as the professor chuckled behind him.

During his first years at university Bill felt at home in the world of the rational. The easiest thing to do was cast alleged spirits and inexplicable connections aside as supernatural phenomena, but that changed the deeper he got into his studies and after the expedition he was certain the world of logic was not sufficient in itself as explanatory model. He turned the professor.

"I realize asserting myself is a practically impossible task in the research world when the demand is to expose something intellectually that isn't intellectual and to cover something which indigenous people don't understand themselves and which they actually aren't interested in understanding."

The professor nodded and looked at him with eyes that contained a hint of pity, as though he were thinking:

You are so right, and: I'm not as bad as you make me out to be. Then he said:

"Don't get me wrong. It's important to tell the stories of how other peoples have lived so we can better understand their reality. But to surrender ourselves to their perception of reality is not our task as anthropologists."

Through the window behind him Bill caught sight of the big swaying trees on the lawn in front of the

Institute, the wind howled around corners. He would like to have said he had finally come to understand the point of departure for spirituality and science were identical because they both were based on a sense of wonder about the world and a playfulness with possible explanations and demanded an open mind and recognition of the paradox as a starting point for human life.

But even though he knew he would regret it, he didn't say another word and left the office. When the heavy wooden door of the building shut behind him the wind took hold of his hair and rustled it and he discovered the light was foggy like mornings of his childhood when he floating pressed his cheek against the cold window pane. Bill descended the wide steps, walked across grass, amongst trees, sensed a hand in his, turned toward a thin man with elongated head, two teeth in his upper, two in his lower mouth, shiny black eyes.

The fever consumed Bill's body and he was shaking all over when the thin man helped him into a pot in which he was boiled until his flesh fell from his bones and afterward the man put his flesh back and gave him an extra rib. Now Bill was no longer the same, he didn't want to be with people and went deep into the forest and talked with animals, until he fell into a deep hole and caught sight of tracks in moist soil, followed them to the river where was a canoe that carried him to the shore opposite where were skyscrapers, cars, buses, thousands of people. He discovered people couldn't see him and entered a house where a family was sitting around a table eating. Bill was hungry and took a lump of boiled meat. One of the son's wondered out loud where the food was disappearing to and the father summoned the local shaman who was bill's own father. He was happy to see Bill but also troubled and rushed to accompany him to the cliff across the river from where he flung him out into empty space.

It was as though he had been floating around ever since and until now hadn't noticed the little house on the island at periphery of the desert, the pine trees, the chair on the terrace, he sensed the taste of coffee, cigarettes, opened his eyes.

The rays of the sun coming through trees hit him, a propeller-driven aircraft passed at low altitude. Bill stood and went into the house and when he stepped through the door to the living room, the person he initially had been penetrated, in a brief flash, through the shield with which he had armored himself, manifested seethingly in the core of his brain. That's how you re-enter the world, he thought, and the feeling got stronger until it transformed to the opposite and he felt the sense of debilitation like a sudden emerging disease. Now he caught sight of Jonas who was sitting at table, the sun drew barred windows on the floor. Jonas was sleeping with his head tilted back, his mouth open, the clock on the wall above the three-legged oven ticking. Bill stepped toward him, placed his hand on his arm and saw himself through Jonas's eyes, the figure, silhouetted by rays of the sun, and the hand dissolved, the sun went away, heavy drops landed on the roof and Bill flowed into the oozing darkness.

WORLD MOTHER

Barbara saw the trees take each other by the arms and move in direction of the house with heavy strides, the ground shaking, windows vibrating, thin coal flakes rustling deep within the chimney. Her body was frozen in place, trembling, she couldn't escape her nature, the drive to digest sad circumstances of others like a world mother, even though she understood with her intellectual capacity the only benefit that might come of it was postponement of those life processes humans weren't always able to identify, all the while her heart gradually dissolved in a hostile world with monitored optimization of productivity, adaptability, cost control, technology enthusiasm, contrast fixation. She had become a product on the stock exchange of market logistics where space for normality was stiflingly cramped, which is why when things got too stressful and she was overwhelmed with tension headaches, on the verge of desperation, she would escape to ... stop!!

She turned her palms to the ocean and the trees ceased their advancement, floating weightlessly, lacking memory, confused and enfeebled there, connected

to earth, enthusiastic to be alive and remembering
everything there.

Jonathan

Barbara was convinced she had blown out the candle before going down to the sea, before she found the flint rock that resembled the island to a T, before she removed her clothes and went out into the splashing water, the offshore wind, swaying seagulls, high clouds, dusty sun, before she hurled herself forward, dove down to the bottom and quickly came back up. The water was perhaps 15 degrees, her skin tightened, her heart pounded, before she took her clothes under her arm, returned to the house, went through each room, placed the stone on the windowsill next to the candle holder and noticed a square note on the dining table: "Shopping list" it said. Had she left the list there in her absentmindedness? The refrigerator was gapingly empty, she shrugged it off and discovered she was naked, found the string shopping bag under the kitchen table and blew out the candle.

A short moment later Barbara entered the supermarket through the glass door, grabbed a shopping basket and took out the list. Was that really her handwriting? She needed eggs, crisp bread, butter, black currant marmalade.

"We've got some good wine on sale, surplus stock."

She turned around toward the young man, ponytail, his sleeves rolled up, who, completely on his own initiative, began talking about the various possibilities as they made their way to the wine section. He was about a head taller than her, slim, had broad shoulders and strong arms.

"Have you moved here to the island?"

His voice didn't sound like that of a young man, it was soft and full like the television host of a children's show of the past.

"I'm renting a summerhouse."

"In connection with work?"

"No."

"So you're on vacation, then?"

She couldn't help smiling at all his questions.

"You could call it that," she said and was just about to add he should just continue asking her questions, because his voice was so pleasant to listen to.

And she'd answer everything.

"This one is good, it's aromatic and at the same time velveety," he said.

An older woman stepped into the shop and headed

toward the kiosk by the cash registers. The young man went over to attend to her.

"What did she get?" Barbara asked when he stood in front of her again.

"You're certainly curious," he said, smiling.

"Like certain other people."

"Well, if you must know: the morning paper, aspirins, a lotto coupon, cheroots and two non-alcoholic beers."

"Okay."

"I grew up here on this island and attended high school on the mainland. Right now I'm writing my Master's thesis at the university. When I'm not taking care of my mother."

"Is she sick?"

"She's soon going to die, she says, and I think she may be right."

"What is she suffering from?"

"I don't know. She refuses to get examined, much less hospitalized. She tends to be very independent but has given me permission to dispense her painkillers."

He caught sight of a customer waiting by the cash register and Barbara watched him as he left, bluish flames smoldered around the periphery of his body, she shook the vision away. A short while later he returned.

"I'll take two, she said.

"You don't have to buy anything." She placed the bottles in the basket.

"Where is the summerhouse located?" he asked.

"Out toward the water, a kilometer in that direction."

"I know where that is."

"Yes, I think you delivered some items the other day."

They walked up to the cash register.

"My name's Jonathan," he said.

She was almost back at the house when she realized she hadn't bought any food, she went straight home, opened a bottle of wine and took it outside with her in the sun.

GOD

Bill had felt cold to the bone and lit the wood stove, and it was already too warm in the low-ceilinged living room when Mie unexpectedly knocked on the door. She was standing at the front door wearing lipstick, high-heeled shoes and looked like she was leaning up against the evening twilight. The young girl in the ice cream parlor smiled and winked at him, had hired a babysitter, asked him if he'd offer a glass of wine. They drank wine from the supermarket, talked about supernatural phenomena, Mie's life in the service of Christianity, having children with three different men, the latest arrival with a man from the southern hemisphere. She dreamed of moving down to him with the whole bunch, but mama had forbidden it. The family lived according to decrees of the clergy and Mie had arrived with a baggage full of sins, activated a buried joy of life and power of display, and now they hadn't seen each other for six months.

"That's my small human life," she concluded, placing her hand on Bill's knee. "So, what about yours?"

"What about my small life?"

The heat from the stove oven produced pearls of sweat on his forehead. She got up and extended arms and Bill envisioned her on a pulpit.

"No matter how lonely and lost we feel we are, and this is a verified fact, part of something bigger, an entirety that is meaningful at the same time it is unfathomable, an all encompassing, omnipresent force which I don't know what is, but which I will, to give it a recognizable name, call God."

"Hearing you say that makes me long for the wilderness even more. I've seldom been so happy to be alive as when I was out there."

"So, what did you find there?"

"A kind of self-evident, simple life. Which, nevertheless, is based on a cosmology that's complex. There are many dangers. Natural phenomena can kill you, bears can kill you, and you can die of starvation or in an accident, but you're never scared of anything and very seldom frustrated or confused and you never feel lonely."

"That's exactly what I'm saying. We're never alone, and reminding ourselves of that can be a consolation of sorts."

"You don't understand what I mean. My whole being would look forward to the meal awaiting me, or to sleep close to others in the tent so we could keep warm and when I woke I'd be as excited as a little kid to find whether any animals had been caught in the traps, or whether one of the reindeer had had calves in the course of the night. Everything was natural in the most beautiful manner you can imagine, as opposed to life here where nothing gives way because everything is problematized and analyzed to death, everyone is fed on skepticism and distrust, and even love between people is a sad study in self-destruction."

Mie was about to say something but let her hands fall and Bill observed her as she unbuttoned his pants.

She took of all her clothes and stood naked in front of him until he pulled her down on his lap and they gently kissed, then hard, and she moved in slow, circular movements until they slid to the floor and made love in front of the stove oven. Mie was now lying next to him on the hard floor and breathing heavily as Bill's hand moved across her body, he thought of the last time he had made love with his ex.

They were lying underneath a undulating sheet

and he could have gone on and on, and she asked for a break before she lay back down on the bed with her legs spread and her arms extended to the side. Bill's body still knew what to do and even though he was out of shape he quickly got back into it. First it was his ex lying under him and moaning, then Mie, then his ex, then Mie, then his ex, Mie, his ex, Mie.

She left at around 2 a.m., the stove oven moaned loudly due to all the heat. Bill's hip was in pain and he massaged it with a numbing cream, her scent, Mie's scent, vibrated all around him when he fell asleep under the blanket on the couch. He woke with the sun, stretched creakingly, and took a bath.

Bill stepped out of the bath, dried himself, looked at his body's reflection in the misty mirror, the stubs and bags on his face. He would have preferred returning to the tiny death of sleep, to a world where Jonas and his ex-wife existed. Jonas was already one with the gigantic whirl of orbit. Bill was to see his sons again, but they wouldn't be able to recognize him and when he introduced himself they would smile forthcomingly and think showing up at a private event like that one, was perhaps a bit pushy.

Bill made his stomach hard and slapped with the palm of his hand. It had disappeared during the course of his trip but had started to bulge out a little again. His index finger grazed across the uneven scars which in varying depths cut down into his skin, he held his hands in front of his face, sun spots had started to appear and the stubborn hairs on his fingers were thinning out. He straightened his back, left the bathroom in rapid strides and pulled on his clothes.

Bill put the summerhouse behind him and wandered out into the desert, settled at the top of one of the hills, the sun was shining, the wind cooling everything down, far in the distance the mountains of clouds kissed the face of the sky and he felt as though everything repeated itself but in new ways and didn't understand where the door that had opened within him had been hidden, he pushed down the door handle and stepped into a world he knew so well, where the life his ex and he had for fifteen years had played out. He had returned from the wilderness on Monday and she had left him Wednesday morning. She took her life seriously, he made note of it, didn't want to be a victim of his inability to disengage himself. She exuded certainty, found a new love and needed to sweep all affection aside.

She hadn't done it to punish him, he had triggered it on his own.

Bill let his gaze get lost in the heavens, he asked for a stream of insights but the questions vanished like screams of the seagulls, tracks in the desert sand and there was no response, his brain just went into overdrive, a staticky radio hitting a new channel, the gas flame lit, water poured into a pot that landed on the stove, her figure grazed his field of vision, and he fell into the bottomless well of consciousness, registered frequencies in everything upon which he focused his attention, swung in similar frequencies as those with whom he encountered, perhaps everything was pre-destined, everything.

Taking Off

They were to meet at the hot dog stand by the harbor. Barbara got there too early, sat by the edge of the harbor throwing gravel into black water, small fish swam in circles on the surface. She started freezing and turned her face to the sun. Mie called her name. Where the hot dog stand had been there was now a fish restaurant where Mie would pick up the dish "Shooting Star" and french fries for the kids, she explained, as they sat across from one another at the table with the red and white chequered tablecloth and drank local beer, dark as top soil, retold their past in a compromised version and Barbara, who would have preferred fish and chips had to admit the "Shooting Star" dish was exceptionally good.

The sun evaded the curtain and hit Mie's face, her skin smooth and dark brown, her teeth white and even just as they were back then. Did she remember how they used to lie on a blanket in the hollow in the dunes and Barbara had placed her hand on her lap? The material of the bikini had rustled. Did she remember she had kissed Barbara with her tongue?

She had tasted like strawberries they had just eaten. Afterward, Barbara had been ashamed, later she grew warm inside when she thought about it and later on the experience transformed itself to a small bubble of joy which burst within her every so often.

"I sometimes think about the dangerous things we used to do back then," Mie said at the same moment.

Barbara caught her gaze.

"Yes?"

"Like the time we sailed in my parent's row boat without life vests."

"And without anyone knowing about it."

"Or when we ran across the runway just before a plane landed."

Mie held up her hand in front of her face and shielded her eyes from the sun. Was she also thinking of that afternoon on the beach? Perhaps she had forgotten.

"Not to mention when we ran around in people's yards and spied on them?" Mie continued.

"Yes, and we kept long journals about what they did."

There was a moment of silence.

"How are you doing?" Mie asked.

"Are you ready to perform some grief therapy?"

"Always."

"My strategy has been to place all unpleasant things in an inaccessible spot in the mind."

"And does that work?"

"No, not very well. I don't think there's room for more."

She told Mie about the time she switched from the subject of physics to the subject of medicine and shortly afterward met the man she would marry. Twelve years later she opened her own medical practice, had a beautiful house, skied in tall mountains, surfed on high waves, enjoyed the sun on the Pacific islands until it all came to an end and the house was sold, the platinum card lost in the chaos of moving, her migraines started, she sold her medical practice, bought an apartment and lived off the proceeds, gradually started to feel better, had brief affairs that didn't mean anything, didn't trust men her own age, corrupted by an upbringing without masculine role models, with mothers whose goal in life was to flourish on the same conditions as their husbands, only more efficiently because they were more uncompromising, more accommodating to the fascistic societal structures that had settled across the world like a corrosive blanket of oppression which from generation to generation became increasingly difficult to get rid of.

The imprint was ingrained in her and she could do nothing about it. For a long time it was always dark outside and the fear of going mad struck her like a blow to the chest, a hand that closed its callous fingers around her heart and squeezed until she lost consciousness.

"I think I know what you mean," said Mie.

"Are your parents alive?"

Mie shook her head.

"Dad died five years ago during the fall. My little sister has moved back together with her husband and kids and taken over the house."

"Is the annex still there?"

"They use it for storage. What about your mother?"

"She's still working. She got divorced from my step-father many years ago and lives alone now."

They sat for a short while not saying anything.

"What happened to your dad was terrible. Everyone on the island was talking about it. We still talk about it," said Mie.

Barbara felt like telling her what happened in the wake of his death but didn't have the energy for it, she sensed how it still managed to play out in her mind, and she told Mie the story about the time she moved in with her mother and step-father. They had already gotten the first son and the next one came the following year.

Barbara decided to live with her father after the divorce which her mother had interpreted as a rejection of her which it also was but only because she didn't like her mother's new husband. Barbara became the ugly duckling no one took any interest in, she managed on her own, got into boarding school and moved away from home in the middle of high school. When she later told people about her life with the new family they pitied her. It must have been extremely hard, traumatizing, and degrading for her, and practically a miracle that she didn't perish altogether. But she refused to be a victim with an accompanying success story. In light of all the evilness that took place in the world, losing one's father and not being loved by one's mother were luxury problems. Furthermore, it had seasoned her and equipped her with mental strength and a strong sense of survival. The resulting excessive desire to please was something she could have done without and the never failing guilt conscience for being, however false it was, the root cause of everyone's suffering.

Mie placed her hand on Barbara's and gently squeezed it and Barbara regretted voicing her lamentations out loud.

"Life's a bitch and then you die. Isn't that how the saying goes?"

Barbara nodded, attempted to look serious and they both laughed and then Mie lifted her hand up to her mouth and kissed it.

"I've missed you in my life," she whispered.

"I've also missed you but didn't realize until now."

She nodded and they sat for a moment looking at each other.

"Have you seen the guy we ran into in the desert? Wasn't there love in the air?" Barbara then asked.

"That's overdoing it, I think," Mie said, blushing.

"You don't have to say more."

"I already have a boyfriend."

"Yes, down south."

"I think we'll move in together someday. But his

mother isn't enthusiastic and the mothers decide everything down there."

"Well, there's no harm in having a little fun with... Bill?"

"I just hope I don't fall in love with him."

"Do you think you could?"

"Maybe just a little."

BEAR

What it was exactly that had taken place just before he crashed down the hill, much less at the very moment of the accident, Bill wasn't sure as he lay on the gurney in the doctor's clinic clad in a hospital gown and elastic bandage around his elbow, receiving a tetanus vaccination, a horse pill prophylactic penicillin. On that particular day he had gone in the exact opposite direction of the desert, he wanted to climb a steep slope, a small mountain. He wasn't as physically fit as he had been and was forced to take breaks so when he discerned the contours of a bench at the top he envisioned how he'd recover with a cigarette if he had remembered to take the pack with him, of course, and stuck his hand in his pocket. The next thing he remembered was opening his eyes halfway, the fog gradually dissolved, the sun light, white cloud formations, blue sky, a warm breath of air on his face, something moist grazing his forehead, a brown fur animal that smelled of fish, a bear.

He evaded breathing, it might give up the game with its fatal ending, as bears were known for appreciating.

Like cats, they dosaged the torture, kept the prey alive, postponed the pleasure, the act of killing, the scratchy tongue returned, now the cheeks, the mouth, the nose, the ears, bears loved salt, the fishy taste between the lips.

"There you are, you rascal."

Bill saw a figure bend over him and felt a hand on his shoulder.

"What's happened to you?" the voice asked.

A friendly face appeared.

"Where's the bear?"

The man laughed briefly, squatted.

"It's just a horse, a mischievous one that likes to wander off sometimes."

A humming feeling moved up through his body, a branch was swaying in the wind. Bill's feet were buzzing, his legs, his abdomen, his stomach area, his chest, his neck, his head were whirling, drama— thoughts, the blinding dominance of randomness, the streaming rivers of life that dried out, the screams of a toiling heart from the abyss.

The body shook itself free of thought categories, the experiences of the creature in amniotic fluid.

"Are you in pain?" the man asked. "Take my hand and try to sit up."

Bill got to his feet, tried to regain balance.

"Did you really think it was a bear?"

Bill nodded.

"I was in close contact with one once."

"Bear, that's what I'll call him from now on. Are you able to walk?"

"I'm a little dizzy," Bill moaned.

"Let's get you over to the clinic. By the way, my name's Morten and I'm a doctor here on the island."

"And you were just out walking with your horse?"

"That's correct. Young animals demand a lot of exercise. I had to take a call on my phone and was inattentive for one moment and then he wandered off."

He shaped his hands into a horse shoe and helped Bill into the saddle.

"I don't feel entirely confident about this. Can the horse really carry me?"

"Don't worry. He's as strong as an ox. Or should I say a bear" he added. "This is his baptism as a riding horse and you and he will be forever bound to each other."

"Does that mean he has never before had a human in the saddle?"

"I have ridden on and trained him, you're the first besides me to ride him."

"That's no consolation, maybe it'd be better if I walked?"

"Just hold on to the bit and I'll hold the reins, there's no reason to be nervous. Let's start back."

A sharp twinge on the back of his neck, his elbow, the gravel road on the way to town, people who observed the procession, a sense of deep gratitude the doctor had passed by and discovered him. Morten pulled the horse into the fold, helped Bill safely off the horse and supported him into the clinic. Shortly afterward he was lying on this gurney here as he watched the doctor work meticulously with his tweezers.

"Counting twenty-four ticks."

Morten placed yet another tiny black insect next to the others on the white sheet and placed the tweezers on the steel table.

"If Bear hadn't found me ..."

"You'd probably still be lying there," he interrupted. "Come back in a few days and let me know how you're doing."

The Third Creature

Bill was in his bed below the slanted window, looked at the telephone that looked as though it was floating above the duvet, no messages, he let it fall and the blue light disappeared shortly afterward.

He heard his own laughter from somewhere far in the distance, the darkness stared through the window, reached out toward him, grabbed hold of his shoulders, shook him. Bill got up, the shooting pain in the back of his neck radiated up to his brain when he walked down the stairs, out to the bathroom, back to the kitchen, placed the glass on his lips and let the cold water circulate in the cavity of his mouth. His emotions were starting to move up through his heart to his head, floating down his body like the sun moving across the sky, changed colors over and over to finally retreat into the darkness, taking it with him like the warm wind that encompassed him every time he stepped out of the house. He spoke with people he knew and was certain the imprint of his words reached them no matter where they were, one moment he was breathing here and the next moment somewhere else that vibrated around him like an invisible cover. He was in a small propeller airplane and the island had just started to appear in the distance when an explosion enveloped him, tore his body to pieces, and a shrill alarm could be heard in the distance. The blue light was activated, he got a hold of the telephone, it was Mie so he let it ring, he had to find his legs, liberated people liberate each other so they can live out their dreams. It was something Mie could have said.

*

Somehow it had become morning, and the sun hit Bill's legs through the slanted window as he wandered around in a distant past in his first apartment in the city. For two years nothing happened except that time continued to pass, which it did in great quantities, and it was lonely. He envisioned he would enter a full-blown relationship with a woman with whom he would one day cohabit if he were to be so lucky. He quickly foresaw the emergence of a third, an invisible persona who would become increasingly more vigorous with its own operating system, nourished by energy supplies from both of them, its own identity that would lose its way when they were apart from one another. At which point it would stick out its head and demand things it couldn't get. And if it didn't work out in the end, the essence of what they had would never disappear because their core had once and for all melted together in the landscape of eternity, beyond limitations of thought, emotions and consciousness.

Bill sat up in bed. Maybe it had been necessary for him to have his heart broken because it sent him out into the solar system for an indefinite period of time which would provide a vantage point from which he could observe the coherent organism all living things were one with before finally landing on the island alone in order to acknowledge that there are no words for it and perhaps even to discover his belief that the key to the door in the endlessly tall wall separating him and the future did indeed exist.

Barbara was starving, she needed fish and chips and it took her 15 minutes to reach the restaurant whereupon she found the bench with a view across the deserted marina, soft, warm fish meat enveloped in a crispy dough, sprinkled with vinegar, salt potato wedges, homemade remoulade.She stretched, the contents of the dish resulted in fatigue and increasing dizziness which she, stretched out on the white boards, knew was a harmless reaction on account of her blood sugar. The reaction gradually subsided, she sat up, dozed in the sun while a couple of boys played ball against the wall, the ball hit a lock and got off course, landing at her feet. She grabbed hold of it, threw it back with a well executed back hand that triggered a piercing pain in her arm, wear and tear, the count down.

One of the boys sprinted for the ball which had once again gotten off course, stumbled and disappeared over the edge of the pier, a splash could be heard. Barbara jumped up and ran and stared down into the foaming, dark water.

"Get your friend's parents," she shouted to the boy

who stood paralyzed and she slipped off her shoes, tore off her sweater and jumped in, ignored the sense of shock, the fish and potatoes on their way back up.

She filled her lungs and dived in but the boy was nowhere to be seen; the current must have taken him, it was pulling and tearing at her. Something lay at the bottom, red sneakers, she grabbed hold of a leg and pulled the lifeless body to her. His eyes were closed, his mouth half open. She held the boy with one of her arms and swam upward with the other, broke through the surface of the water and shouted for help. A face immediately appeared, it was one of the waiters from the restaurant. He lay down, stretched out his arms and lifted the boy. Barbara caught sight of the steps in the wooden construction of the pier and swam over to it, and shortly afterward she was on the pier where the waiter was standing holding the boy in his arms.

"I don't think he's breathing. What do we do?" he shouted in despair.

"I'm a doctor. I need your shirt, he has to lie down on the ground. Did you call 911?"

Barbara searched for the boy's pulse but couldn't find any. It didn't necessarily mean all hope was lost and she knew what she had to do and gave him a cardiac massage and resuscitation interchangeably, she kept thinking, this can't go wrong, not again, I can't let that happen. But he didn't get better and Barbara's heart was pounding so hard she felt as though she might faint as she pressed on his chest and gave him mouth-to-mouth and then finally … finally there was a hint of life, he started to cough and water came out of his mouth, his eyes opened. She wrapped him in a shirt and held him close and he kept on coughing and crying as she stroked his wet hair, kissed his forehead and whispered that everything was going to be okay. Then she caught sight of a man riding a horse that was galloping through the harbor area, he evaded a truck backing up, and for a moment it looked as though the horse was going to toss him off but he managed to stabilize it and then he reached them, slipped down to the asphalt and tied the horse to a bicycle rack.

"I'm the doctor on this island. What happened?" he asked slightly out of breath, his hand on Barbara's shoulder.

"The boy fell into the harbor and I got him out. I gave him cardiac massage. He's breathing again."

The doctor squatted and took over and Barbara felt a sense of gratitude spread through her body and then she started shaking and crying, hiding her face in her hands. The doctor examined the boy and talked to him and he said his name was "Felix" and told him how old he was, "eight" and, finally, the trembling subsided. Barbara wiped her eyes but at that very moment the sound of a female voice shouting could be heard and the boy started whimpering again.

"Felix, Felix!" the voice sobbed and the woman collapsed on the pier and received the boy's wet body.

"Your boy is going to be okay. He's had a shock, but he's okay," the doctor said reassuringly.

He got up with some difficulty and walked over to Barbara. He was somewhere in his 50's, slim, reached her chin, looked at her with a smile which she interpreted as appreciative.

"And what about the life-saver, is she okay too?" he asked.

Barbara nodded.

"Wet and cold, but okay. The most important thing is ..." She nodded toward Felix and his mother.

"It's a good thing you were around," the doctor said,

taking a few steps toward his horse restlessly trotting in place, its nostrils contracting and expanding and white foam dripping to the asphalt. He patted its muzzle and turned toward Felix's mother.

"You can go home. Give Felix a warm bath and keep an eye on him. I think everything's fine but if he starts to feel unwell call me at once."

"Thank you, Morten," she said and helped the boy to his feet.

"And thank you…"

"Barbara" she said and sensed the woman's burning hand on her arm.

"I don't think I've seen you before. Are you on vacation here?"

Barbara nodded.

"I'm renting a summer house for an extended period." She hesitated. "What a beautiful boy you've got."

Barbara stroked Felix's hair and he looked at her with eyes she felt she already knew.

"That's just what he is. Say thank you to the nice lady, Felix."

Before the boy had a chance to say anything, Barbara

squatted in front of him and took his hands, she made an effort not to start crying again when she said, "There is nothing to be afraid of. You handled it so well, Felix, and now it's time for you to go home and get some rest."

"Yes, but first I'm taking a bath," he said with a frail voice. "Right, Mom?"

Felix's mother took him by the hand and they started walking. After a few steps he turned around and waved and Barbara waved back. She suddenly felt that everything had turned upside down and at that very moment she felt all her strength had left her body. When she closed her eyes she saw Felix at the bottom of the bay, on the pier, in the steel tub, then she lifted him and kissed him back to life. She heard someone clearing their throat, horse hooves hit the asphalt with a metallic sound and she made eye contact with the doctor and saw his outstretched hand.

"I'm going to walk him a little," he said at that moment. "Would you like to accompany us?"

Shortly afterward they were walking side by side through the harbor area. Her clothes stuck to her body but she was no longer freezing, her sense of gratitude continued to radiate through her body and she began to smile, noticing that the doctor was looking at her with surprise.

"The horse-riding doctor," she said at that 'moment and patted the animal on its protruding belly.

"I breed them. When I don't have patients to see to, I've got horses."

They passed the restaurant, the aroma of fried food. Barbara told him what had happened and he praised her for acting so resolutely. It was a long time since she had heard anyone use the word "resolutely." The sun disappeared behind an area of clouds and the asphalt changed colors.

"So you're also a doctor?" he asked, slowed down the pace and removed a piece of algae from her hair. It was already dry and was picked up by the wind.

"I had a medical practice in Copenhagen but it became..."

"Too strenuous in the long run?" he finished her sentence for her. "I know all about that, was there for thirteen years myself, then I came over here and became a human again. But you don't intend to settle down here, do you?"

"I'm starting to like it ... although the silence can be somewhat ... well, deafening."

He smiled and glanced at his watch.

"The clinic is closed for the day. Can I offer you a glass of wine at my place to help calm your nerves?"

"Thanks, I could really use some," she said even though she mostly just felt like going home.

She followed him through the driveway, past the fold where a herd of horses were standing with their heads bent, grazing, their ears quivering when he whistled. Two yellow sea kayaks leaned against the wall of the house.

Morten disappeared in an adjacent room and returned with a jogging outfit which he handed to her and while he got the white wine from the fridge and poured it into glasses she went out to the bathroom, removed her wet clothes and pulled on the jogging outfit.

"Cheers and thank you," he said when Barbara returned. "If it weren't for you that little guy would have drowned. And that would have been a real tragedy for everybody here on the island."

Before she had a chance to say anything he continued:

"So you had your own medical practice?"

"I held out for five years. I was unable to really get

it off the ground, as they say. In my experience that's something you men are much better at, which I found out during my training period. Once my patients were sitting across from me in my own clinic it was impossible to get them out the door. Which meant I wasn't earning enough. That part improved with time, but I also had difficulty with all the fates I encountered. Finally, I was forced to regard them as wandering cardboard cut-outs of sorts until I myself became one in the end, and that just couldn't go on."

"I know what you're saying. The work load is way out of proportion. More and more doctors are getting hit with stress and dying from it, yet still society refuses to acknowledge the fact doctors are also people who have certain limitations. No, indeed, we're not cardboard cut-outs, as you say, but we do what's expected because we're all a damn bunch of pleasers."

"Who at the same time have to struggle to get people to understand why they shouldn't believe the conspiracy theories they come across in shady social platforms. The value of our professional knowledge is gradually losing its credibility in people's eyes. Our need to help others is subject to suspicion because they immediately assume we're sitting in the pockets of big pharma. Which is true of some."

"I haven't been subject to that kind of suspicion when dealing with my patients, at least not on this island. What worries me more is the sense of apathy I see amongst my colleagues. I think it's due to the fact social criticism has been replaced by self-criticism and a sense of shame of not having lived up to one's own twisted ideals. Every man for himself, as the mantra goes, we're not to be dependent on one another, which is totally absurd because the only way we can be anything in the world is by virtue of one another. Something you demonstrated in the most heroic way."

"Wouldn't you have done the same thing?"

"One never knows."

He fidgeted restlessly and looked at his watch.

"I better go out to the horses."

He got up and Barbara followed him. At that moment the front door opened and a man with braided beard, wearing shorts and jogging shoes, entered. Morten went to greet him and they quickly kissed.

"Barbara, this is my husband, Morten," said Morten.

"Morten and Morten," she said, squeezing his big hand.

The recently arrived Morten waved at her and disappeared up the stairs to the first floor where the shower was turned on shortly afterward.

"You know, I could use a stand-in every now and then," said Doctor Morten when they were standing in front of the house. "Would you be interested do you think?" A horse neighed and he whistled at it.

"Maybe," she said with hesitation and for the first time in a very long time she felt a budding desire to work.

"Think about it and stop by the clinic tomorrow if you have time."

Life in the Forest

Barbara balanced on the ridge of the roof, the slanted window was wide open to the left of her. She sat on the roof which she could use as a roller coaster, let go with her hand and allowed the weight to distribute itself onto her legs. When she closed her eyes the light came sailing through the quivering water particles of the clouds, birds started singing, black patches in the sky joined into one cohesive blackness. She stepped among the trees, the scent of spruce, decomposing tree trunks, rotten leaves, dead bodies that were being digested by living bodies. Some rustling could be heard from the forest floor, light through the branches. She turned toward the house, a woman sitting in an armchair in front of the window, a steaming cup, moved the crumbs from the crispbread in her lap to the tile-topped table, the sound of shrill tires on the opposite side of the trees, a resilient forest floor, needles pricks between the forehead and temporal lobes, thoughts emerging like colonies of baby monkeys, the trees grew taller, more condensed. Her forehead caught the ray of sun through the roof of the branches, joyful moments, rustling leaves on the curb, a blackbird basking with its broken wing and looking at her with eyes wide open. She found a stone the size of her hand, lifted the cup to her lips, a joyful summer's day in the baby carriage beneath the floating arms of the birch tree, trembling in the borderland between the vast ocean of the sky, the birds' singing, the insects' buzzing about, the scent of grass, flowers, a joyful moment beneath the sky, at one with the body of the birch tree, with wind, everything that was and everything that would be, joyful on the beach under the sun, her life in his, his in hers. She dug a hole in the bottom of the forest for the blackbird, covered it with soil, sprinkled a couple of leaves on top and placed a wreath of cones.

Battlefield

Bill set two pillow-covered plastic chairs on the planks of the terrace, spongy from moisture, the cigarette pack on the inserted table of rare wood, brought to an accessible height with the help of eight volumes of encyclopedia, next to the ashtray, canned beers, magazines. He leaned back, the injured arm in his lap, a burned-out cigarette, a pinched nerve in his left foot, loose ankle joints, pains in his knee from his time out in the wilderness, aches in his coccyx from years of sitting in front of a screen on a miserable office chair, a carpal tunnel arm, creaking wrist joints, the inability to move certain fingers, the good effect that painkillers had as long as he didn't move the back of his neck too much. He realized the aging men, uncles, professors who had encouraged him to appreciate the lack of concern that came with youth, the full functionality of his organism, the accelerating force of his brain, had all been right.

Bill hadn't listened. Not until his body began showing signs of debilitation had he understood that for the rest of his life he would have to adjust to its ever-increasing decline.

An airplane was approaching. The airport was situated a couple of hundred meters away, a grass blanket in the desert and when wind came from a certain direction, or so he assumed, the planes always passed by that way. It was a two-engine plane, he could tell by the way it growled as though it wanted to put everyone and everything in its place and remind all the birds not to take flight. Bill noticed his heart was pounding hard against his chest, and he lit a cigarette at the same time his father across time lit a cigarette and coughed, making a hole in the smoke cloud, and said now it was Bill's turn and his fingers wrapped themselves around the cold steering wheel. Behind him his mother and little brother were chit-chatting, he couldn't hear what they were saying. The vibration of the engine slid through his arms, planted itself on his shoulders and he felt a bubbling sense of pride when his father praised him for keeping the aircraft on an even course. The island emerged in the horizon, the small figure on the big blue ocean resembled the premature fetus in the book on pregnancy that his mother kept in the bookshelf and he was given permission to turn the steering wheel, making the airplane careen slightly before his father took over, letting it drop through strata of air, making his stomach tickle.

Shortly afterward they were hovering over summerhouses, the machine hit the grass blanket and soon they were all four running through the desert to the dunes, the beach, threw off their clothes and hurled their naked bodies into the clear water.

Bill tried to recall what had happened the time his parents had gone out to the airport without them. Why weren't he and his little brother going to join them like they usually did? It was a Saturday, in the middle of the day. The sun was shining, Bill was standing by the window and watched as they left with his little brother who was to stay the night at his friend's house at the other end of town. Before his mother got into the car she stood for a long time looking toward the window and the curtain behind which he was hiding. Did she have a premonition of what was going to happen? Bill pressed his cheek against the window pane and sensed the coldness spread to his chin, nose, further to his shoulders and the top of his back. After they had disappeared, he walked past four houses down the street to Jonas' place. They were going to grill with his parents and have beef sandwiches, hot dogs, soda and he and Jonas were going to sleep in the tent in the yard. During the afternoon they had rolls and tea under the canopy when a police officer showed up by the gate to the street. Jonas's father spoke with him for what felt like an eternity and looked very serious when he got Bill and told him that there had been an accident. Bill's little brother was already sitting in the backseat of the police car.

What happened afterward was very hazy. At one point they were standing together with their grandmother and grandfather in front of an ice cream parlor and were given permission to choose whatever they wanted. They chose a Popsicle even though they would rather have had one of the big waffles with whipped cream and jam, and they ate it on the piece of grass along the water.

After living at Jonas's place for a while, Bill woke in a strange house, ate his meals with strangers, attended a different school while everything in him was screaming for the light his parents had shared, and for the sense of belongingness he had with his little brother who didn't get along with his foster family, ended up at an institution and later traveled to a village by the sea where he met a local girl and settled down, became a carpenter and built houses.

That was all that Bill knew because they never spoke about their past and Bill didn't want to dwell on the fact that he considered the years subsequent to their parents' death as being synonymous with the scenes from a horror movie, the horrendous impression of which had been imprinted in his mind where they would never be removed. It wouldn't be until he was close to dying from starvation in a hunter's cottage in the wilderness that he started to comprehend the violent events that had impacted his life, his childhood, weren't permanent, destructive crystalizations implanted in his mind per se but could perhaps be, if he allowed it, constructive insights instead and it was at that point he decided that if he came out of the wilderness alive he would go back to the island and allow it to happen.

When they were children they wanted to be pilots, he and his little brother, but things didn't turn out that way and the airplane was now visible, and it was indeed a two engine plane sailing low across the trees, swaying lightly, and it occurred to Bill that where others sensed what they wanted and acted on those feelings and sensations, Bill tended to do the opposite. As if it had been written in the tale of his destiny, life was a battlefield upon which bloody battles were constantly fought. But it couldn't go on like that.

THE LAST DAY

Bill didn't tell anyone he had been abandoned by his wife, had feigned having a bad flu and sought leave from the university. A colleague said when you are out traveling your destination moves further away and it becomes evident that the journey itself was the actual destination. Bill pretended to have understood the connection, but what journey and what destination? He wanted to step out from the shadows of tragedy to finally become an adult and acknowledge his own worth and stand by it but a force kept pulling him in the opposite direction.

Was that the source of which he was possessed, what he had to offer the world? And if he were to cut off the cord to his own self-destruction derived from his childhood years, would he then be left with nothing? What did he have to offer if the experiences and the way in which he grappled with them could no longer be used? One thought led to another and a web of memories pulled him away from the present moment he was trying to hold on to. He wanted to love himself and his wanderings in a meaningless world but he was struggling, so instead he opened a can of beer, lit a cigarette, the warmth of sun mixed with cool breezes from the sea, crackling grains of sand between his teeth, the butterflies drawing nectar from dandelions, undulated with their soft, white wings and brought him to safety in the eye of the sun. But far away a scream moved like waves through the haze of warmth.

LITTLE BROTHER

Bill's little brother was screaming somewhere in the house and he jumped down the stairs to see to him and tripped on the last step and fell in front of the door to the children's room and hit his face on the floor.

Blood was running from his mouth when he lifted his head and checked with his tongue. One of his front teeth was gone. At that very moment his father came running, picked up the tooth and looked at Bill who was pointing toward the door.

"He's just hysterical. Get a cloth and wipe away the blood before it seeps down through the floor boards," he said in a tired voice.

Behind the door his little brother was screaming. Bill's heart pounding wildly, or was it his little brother's fists pounding against the floor? Bill sat down in front of the door.. The sun coming through the gable window shone on his cheek and gradually the screaming subsided into a soft whimpering sound like the dog would make when it was dreaming. Bill fell asleep and woke when his father unlocked the door and announced he had made an appointment at the dentist's for the following day so they could remove the stump and the grown-up tooth could properly replace it and now it was bedtime. He lifted his brother from the floor, tucked the duvet under him.

Many years later he found a match box in the drawer of his father's writing desk. "Bill" and a date had been written on it. Inside the box was the front tooth and Bill wondered whether his father ever looked at it and what went through his mind.

It was in those years when Bill and his little brother slept in the same room and had to be in bed by eight o'clock and one night a sweet aroma drifted up the stairs at the same time their mother's voice rang through the ceiling.

Bill couldn't hear what she was saying but their father's response was now rumbling like an earthquake. He envisioned that they were standing across from one another in the work room, encompassed by tobacco smoke below the black roof beams.

"I have to pee," Bill's brother whispered.

"Then go down and pee."

"You have to come with me," he whimpered.

They tip-toed down the stairs, avoided the step

halfway down the stairs that creaked and the next to last one as well, which was even worse, the scent of spring rolls had become stronger, he sat down and peed, still sniffling.

"Do you think they're going to get a divorce?" Bill's brother asked when they were back in their beds.

"Of course not."

"We're the ones they're fighting over, Mom said our names just before when we were walking up the stairs."

Bill had also heard it.

"They're not getting divorced."

His brother started to cry, a faint sobbing that sounded like rain drops landing on the metal covering of the bay window. They finally fell asleep to wake a moment later to the scent of toasted soft rolls, the Sunday summer sun penetrating cracks in the curtains and for a few brief moments he truly believed everything had changed but then he heard his mother's icy voice from the hallway and he didn't understand what she meant when she said:

"You move from person to person, and each time you take what you need and move on. You are a battery that has to be recharged and it happens totally automatically."

Bill sat bent over forward and was breathing heavily. Already before they disappeared he had lost his way and had been roaming about in search of himself in a reality he couldn't seem to be at home in where people, in desperation and despair, showered one another with malice. He fidgeted with his feet and the tears drew a chaotic pattern on his pants.

The Landscape of Eternity

"Leave me alone already."

The light child's voice moved in waves through the water. Barbara pushed algae aside, swam in direction of the red sneakers, hesitated for a moment, caught the boy's eye when he floated away, a rock in the universe, the trail through the forest, the roaring of the ocean, aromatic pine needles, red ants, gnarled branches, the dunes way ahead, silence, sleep, they played with stones at the shore, fought, he fell in love, unhappy, collapsed from exhaustion, the trail through the forest, someone crying, Felix.

Barbara sat up and it was pitch black outside, there were no manuals she could look in, no one to give the responsibility to.

Her ex-husband thought, which she herself had most probably also thought, that they would be stronger together apart. She remembered his last words to her:

"This isn't about you not being able to manage on your own. We both have to create the life we came here to live, from now on separately."

Barbara felt he was right but that crushed her heart.

She now slid down the armchair in front of the window and let the moonlight rinse him out of her body.

MORE WINE

Morten sat at a folding table in the makeshift kitchen of the medical clinic and was eating an open faced sandwich with tomatoes and onions. He offered one to Barbara but she declined and had a cup of coffee instead.

She was interested in filling in for him a few times a week, something hands-on. Could she start already that afternoon? he asked, because it looked like a mare was just about ready to go into labor. A patient arrived in the waiting room and she took leave of Morten, sauntered to the supermarket and entered the cool premises of the store. A man with sandwich bread, margarine, a weekly journal in his basket was on his way to the cash register. How will I come back to life?

"Running out of wine?" Jonathan asked, his hands at his sides.

"Maybe, got anything you can recommend? I want to try something new."

"I'm not the big wine expert."

"You sounded pretty convincing last time we spoke."

He tried to smile.

"How's your mom doing?"

"The time is approaching, I think, but I'm not sure. She can hardly sleep on account of the pain."

He lowered his voice and it grew slightly softer than usual.

"I'm administrating her pills and have been given strict orders how many she's allowed to take. And every day she asks me to give her the whole package so she can get it all over with."

"Maybe the dosages have to be slightly increased, talk with her doctor about it."

He let out a deep sigh and looked down at his feet.

"I don't know, maybe."

Barbara caught sight of a slightly gray-haired man who was standing with his back to them, bent over the refrigerated counter at the opposite side of the store.

She turned back around toward Jonathan.

"It's not fair for you alone to have to bear the responsibility of your mother. You need to get help," she said in a low voice.

The man stood up straight and placed something in his basket, perhaps a carton of ice cream. Then she saw it was Bill and he immediately caught sight of her and smiled in a somewhat aloof manner, bowed slightly and walked in the direction of the cash register.

She followed him with her eyes.

"She took care of me when I was little and now where she's the one who's little it's my turn to take care of her. That way everything's in balance," Jonathan said with determination in his voice and it seemed to Barbara he grew both in terms of height and width.

Then he took a bottle down from the shelf.

"This one's supposed to be good, a little expensive." He lightly tapped a spotlight in the ceiling that had started to blink and then stopped, he looked at her. "I want to thank you for saving my nephew's life yesterday."

"Is Felix your nephew?"

Jonathan nodded.

"Did you hesitate before jumping into the water to get him?"

"No, I didn't. How is he doing?"

"I paid him a visit yesterday and it was as though he had forgotten all about it. You couldn't tell by looking at him that he had gone through anything."

"That's kids for you."

He smiled.

"I'll take two bottles." She took a deep breath. "And just let me know if you want me to check in on your mother. Did I mention I'm a doctor?"

He smiled to himself, faintly shook his head.

"Thanks, that's nice of you, but she refuses to have any contact with doctors because they oppose her wish to die. And that goes especially for Morten "

"I don't think Morten would actually do that," she said, following Jonathan to the cash register.

He didn't respond.

Bill had long since left the store by the time they reached the cash register. Jonathan replaced the older woman who often sat there, ran the items through, and Barbara placed them in her net shopping bag. Jonathan's hand holding the receipt stopped in the air. The bulging veins resembled overgrown rivers seen from a bird's eye view.

His muscular arms, the tendons on his neck.

"I write poems, or maybe they are more like songs," he said that very same moment.

Barbara's arm froze, she squeezed her wallet, the light flowed through the cracks in the ceiling, the refrigerated display cabinet with cold beverages squeaked, hoarse male voices on the benches in front of the supermarket, the white piece of paper, the bag containing the red wine, the crisp breads, the ingredients for omelet.

"Come by and read them aloud to me," she said without looking back.

Work Is Calling

Barbara took over Morten's warm writing desk chair. It was liberating dealing with something that didn't have anything to do with herself for once, all that soul searching which her stressful state and the accompanying seances at the psychologist's and physical treatments had given rise to. The fatigue, her difficulty concentrating, her sleepless nights, her migraines and pounding heart whenever she tried to fall asleep. There were no scheduled patients and she found a softer chair in the waiting room and was looking at the pictures in the ladies' magazines when the telephone rang and a somewhat sullen voice asked to speak with the doctor due to neck pain.

"You're welcome to come by the clinic, how long have you had this pain? Have you been suffering from any headaches or fever?"

"I've had it for a few days. No fever. Can I come now?"

After a few minutes the door opened, she had forgotten to get his name and social security number, but sure enough, it was the guy from the desert, the supermarket, Bill, who was taller than she remembered him, compact, stubby cheeks, he sat down in the chair across from her.

Barbara's hand was trembling ever so slightly when she received his health insurance card. She looked at it. 46 years old, he looked considerably younger despite his graying hair.

"So we meet again," he said. "You're Mie's friend from the old days. I didn't know you were working as a doctor here on the island."

"Well, I'm not really, I just fill in for Morten when he needs it. I've also borrowed one of his white smocks, as you can see."

She pulled one of the sleeves that didn't reach all the way down to her arm.

"He's no Superman, that's for sure."

They both laughed and she squeezed her hands under the table until they stopped shaking, whereupon she said:

"How can I help you?"

Bill told her he had fallen and had pains in the back of his neck, his shoulder and arm.

"It's important you take it easy," said Barbara. "One

should never take chances with a neck injury. There's always the risk it might be a slipped disc which is not something you want, believe me."

"Morten said something along the same lines."

Barbara positioned herself in back of him and carefully examined his neck muscles.

"Ouch!" he screamed. "Are you sure you're a real doctor?"

She smiled.

"Lie as flat as you can when you're sleeping. That will relieve the pressure on your neck."

"I really don't like lying flat, so I usually prop up the back of my head with pillows. I think I get much better blood circulation that way."

"Quite the contrary, plus you're putting unnecessary pressure on your neck."

"Those are the pro's and con's: either a racing heart or neck pains. And I get a racing heart when I lie flat." "

"That sounds like stress."

"Is is possible to be stressed on this island?"

"Do you have any reason to be?"

"Maybe. I don't know."

"Let's take a closer look at that neck. Take off your

shirt and lie down on your stomach. You can also roll down the top part of your pants."

She pointed at the plank bed covered with gray recycling paper from a roll at the foot of the bed. Bill pulled off his shirt, exposing some deep scars that reached down across his torso from shoulder to his opposite hip.

"I was attacked by a bear," he said before she had time to ask.

"They can be lively."

She let her finger graze a few inches down one of the grooves and stopped because her hand started to shake, it annoyed her.

"You don't have any stitches," she continued.

"It happened way out in the wilderness so there were no doctors close by."

"But I see you managed to avoid getting an infection, you were lucky."

"It wasn't exactly luck. I was traveling with one of the locals who knew melted bear fat prevents infections, so I smeared it on for weeks."

Bill lay down on the plank bed.

"I didn't know doctors gave massages," he mumbled with his face buried in the head holder.

It occurred to Barbara there was something charming about his cheeky manner, his insecurity. She found a bottle of almond oil, heated some between her hands, the clock on the wall ticked. She carefully put pressure along the edge of his cranium, worked through his tendons and muscles that were tense to the bursting, registered that he was muscular, compact, his back strong. She continued down along his spine, and further to his loin, pulled his pants a little further down and massaged the top of his buttocks, before going up toward his shoulders and neck.

"That's it, but stay lying down for a few minutes until you get back to yourself."

Bill immediately sat up, moved his head from side to side.

"That helped. It really did."

He put on his shirt and buckled his belt.

"When can I come back?" he asked, looking as though he regretted his words.

"Just come whenever. That's what we're here for."

The imprint from his hand buzzed in hers when he walked toward the door. There was something different about him from when he entered the clinic before, she followed him with her eyes as he passed the waiting room and disappeared out the door. She would have liked to ask him about his journey. What had happened when the bear attacked? And what was he actually doing here on this island? She discovered she was sitting and smiling. Then she cast a glance at the clock between windows facing the street. She had to hurry to Felix and his family, she hadn't been able to decline their invitation. She would have preferred going straight home to the chair in the sun.

Felix

Felix sat on stairs in front of the door with his blond curls that resembled a cloud of butterflies drawing nectar, wings opening and closing in order to keep their balance in the wind. He caught sight of Barbara and ran to greet her.

"How are you feeling today, Felix?"

"I feel fine."

His blue eyes shone when she lifted him and embraced him.

"Do you want to see my room?"

"Of course."

She followed him into the house and down the narrow hallway that ended at a sweet-sour smelling children's room with a square window that stood ajar, a plank bed that resembled the one she once had, a pull-out desk, laptop.

"Nice cave you got here."

Felix nodded, pulled her over to the bed, turned on his computer and showed her some pictures.

"That's me playing a match, we won 15-0 and I scored six goals."

"You're really good!"

"Yeah."

A pair of red sneakers were lying on the radiator below the window. Barbara moved a bit closer so her thighs touched his. She felt like lifting him up on her knee, holding him, kissing his cheeks, whispering to him they belonged together, but that wouldn't do at all, it would just confuse him.

"That's me and my best friend."

"Was he the one you were playing soccer with down at the harbor?"

"Yes, we're not allowed to do that anymore." His voice turned sad all at once. "We're only allowed to play in my backyard or his. Not in the street, either."

Barbara heard footsteps out in the hallway and the boy's mother appeared at the door, jeans, a loose cowboy shirt.

"Welcome," she said. "Coffee's ready whenever you are."

Felix sighed and folded up his computer, took Barbara by the hand and led her into a low-ceilinged room with dark wooden furniture, a piano with candle holders, rugs, heavy curtains, a whole group of people were looking at her, Felix's father was wearing a one-cover-all with yellow reflexes, his grandmother was wearing a one-size-fits-all gray dress, and his aunt who was wearing a purple nappy wrapped around her hair just like Barbara's mother used to in the distant past. A little while afterward Felix was allowed to go back to his room to play video games.

"We want you to know we are deeply grateful for what you did," Felix's father said in a subdued voice.

Barbara tried to smile. Had she not been there and thrown the ball, the boy would most probably never have fallen in. She answered their questions, dissected sequences, blow by blow.

"Felix has had a shock," Barbara said at one point.

"He doesn't show it," they answered as one.

"An experience like that is always traumatizing to some degree. It's hard to say when the reaction will come, but at some point it will, which is completely natural after something like that happens."

"What kind of a reaction will he get?" Felix's mother sounded worried.

"I can't say. It could be either physical, psychological or a combination of both. It occurs to me it might be good for him to talk to a professional. I'm not a psychologist. But I have plenty of experience working with children in my practice."

"If you think it would help him," she said, with a slight frown.

"Most certainly. Perhaps we can prevent a violent reaction from occurring. I'd like to talk with him alone during the consultations."

The parents looked at one another.

"Okay, we'll send him to you after school," she said.

When the visit was over, Barbara dragged herself through the garden path, turned and looked for Felix in the dark eyes of the window panes. She wished she had been sitting on a bicycle or in a car that could transport her home fast when she heard a voice behind her.

"May I have a brief word with you?"

She turned around to see Felix's aunt whom she had just said goodbye to.

"Of course. What can I do for you?"

"It's about my big sister. Not the one you just met, there are three of us. My oldest big sister is twelve years older than me, she is very sick but she's never been examined to find out what it is. She refuses to. She also refuses to be treated. But then I was thinking maybe you could talk to? It's really hard for all of us watching her suffer so."

"You can't force people to get treatment if they don't want it."

"No, but it's so terrible. She's all alone with everything, she's only got her son, but he's studying and busy. He lives with her, but what can he really do? It's also really hard on him."

Barbara made a snap decision.

"Okay, I'll go see her, but only if she's willing to go along with it. I can make a house call. Talk with her about it and let me know."

"Thank you." Her eyes were moist. "I'll pay her a visit right now and call you afterwards."

Voluntary Death

Bill found himself walking on the beach, crossed the dunes to the camping site and located their spot, a closed space surrounded by pine bushes in the first row from the ocean where they put up tents if the spot was vacant. A camper was parked there now, with a father, mother and two children sitting in metal chairs that caught the sun, busy playing dice so they didn't notice him. He passed by the kiosk sign with pictures of Popsicle, sausages, toast, a man stepped out holding a lotto coupon in his hand. Bill continued across the street and walked toward the white structure which resembled a space ship that could take off from the ground at any moment but it wasn't until he approached the entrance that he remembered there was no one for him to visit. Bill registered a movement behind him, someone came out from the building, a young man walked toward him and said something.

"What did you say?"

"Are you here to see someone?"

Bill shook his head, he tried to smile, rubbed his eyes without wanting to.

"My best friend died the other day. I don't think I've really processed it. What about you?"

"I'm here to see if they have any room for my mom. But everything's taken. They might be able to take her at some point, but it would have to go through a doctor, and she refuses to have anything to do with doctors, or with hospitals, for that matter."

"May I ask why?"

It occurred to Bill he had seen him before. They walked down the street toward the water.

"I think she's afraid of dying at the hospital but she says she refuses to support the profit makers of the death industry and doesn't want to co-finance their yachts, quote unquote."

"But she's willing to got to hospice?"

They were standing at the top of one of the dunes when he turned toward Bill.

"I haven't asked her yet, but a hospice isn't a hospital, of course, and the time is approaching where I'm going to need some assistance."

"Are you taking care of her alone?"

He nodded, whereupon he extended his hand.

"My name is Jonathan."

"Bill," he said, grasping Jonathan's hand.

They reached the shore, the wind was faint and there were hardly any waves. The cloud formation in the sky, which Bill had noticed when he'd been standing in front of the white building, wound its way into the heights like smoke being pulled toward the opening of the tent and he was back in the tent of the reindeer people where Leonid woke him and said it was going to happen now. The smoke stung his throat and eyes when Bill crawled out of his sleeping bag, pulled on his fur outfit and followed Leonid. Someone was shouting somewhere in the camp, a grainy, chanting male voice continued to repeat the same words and Leonid explained it was the one who was ill that was announcing the spirits were calling him. The time had come for the long journey.

"My mother's been sick for almost three years now," Jonathan said at that moment. "It's been hard watching her get worse and worse." He paused. "But I don't feel I can say that because she's the one who's sick and it's much worse for her than me."

"Of course you can. She's your mother and you can't save her. I assume you're talking with someone about all of this?"

"You mean a shrink?" Jonathan asked and shook his head.

"Let's sit down for a moment," said Bill.

"What about your father?" Jonathan shrugged his shoulders.

"He and I don't see each other so often. Dad found someone else a couple of years ago and so my parents divorced. I chose to stay with my mom. But dad lives on the island, too."

"What about your acquaintances?"

"I constantly tried to forget about it when I was studying at university. But I couldn't, of course, and then I felt guilty about leaving her."

"That won't do. You've got a life, too."

"Do I?"

He had tears in his eyes and Bill didn't know what to say so he put his hand on his arm.

"All the time she's been sick I haven't had the wherewithal to talk about it, I didn't want to be 'the guy with the sick mother,' so no one's known about it. Not until recently, when I was forced to tell people I had to take leave in order to take care of her. They had been wondering what became of me." He smiled briefly and Bill nodded.

"So, now they know. At the last minute, you might say. But they all live far away from here. Fortunately I've got a few people who I can talk with by phone." Bill let go of Jonathan's arm.

"That's good. Otherwise ... if you need to talk to an old fart like me about it, just say the word."

"Thanks, that's nice of you, old fart." Bill hesitated before saying,

"I'm an anthropologist and have studied, among other things, the death rituals of indigenous peoples. During winter, I stayed with a tribe in the wilderness way up north."

Bill looked down at his hands. Perhaps it wasn't something a young man felt like hearing. He chewed it over a moment and decided to continue:

"One of the tribe's men was sick. He knew it wasn't long before he was going to die so he demanded to have a final duel with his oldest son so he could leave this world a warrior. In research we call it voluntary death."

"That sounds like a good concept," Jonathan said monotonously. His smile had disappeared and he was looking straight ahead. "Instead of slowly disintegrating."

"I agree," said Bill.

He felt that telling Jonathan what he'd experienced when he and Leonid entered the big tent and positioned themselves at its periphery was the right thing to do. That a bonfire was burning in the center and the family sitting in a circle around the old man and quietly talking. That a reindeer had been slaughtered and that the old man was eating its delicacies, the brains, eyes, marrow. That the people around him were saying they truly loved him and talked about all the important things he'd accomplished in his life. Leonid nodded toward a thin guy of about 15 to 16 years of age who stood with his back toward them holding a spear in his hands and whispered that was the old man's son.

Bill grew silent and they sat a long while looking across the water before Jonathan took a deep breath and said,

"No matter what happened, you'll have to continue."

Bill sighed. He was starting to have second thoughts about whether telling the story to the young man, who was facing an impossible situation, had been such a good idea after all, but he suddenly remembered the dew that had to fall from the grass when rays of sun penetrated the morning fog.

"After everything I've experienced with my mother, I think I can manage hearing about it." He hesitated for a moment. "But I don't have to tell you that. Your friend probably went through something similar."

Bill nodded.

"It took four years before it all ended, but there were also periods when Jonas was doing well and could go back to work. Then the disease re-emerged and he had to get treatment and he'd been declared healthy, then the disease returned,"

Jonathan's voice quivered slightly when he said:

"The big boy was standing with the spear in his hands ..."

"Yes, and then the women and children left the tent and the old man slowly got to his feet," said Bill. "He took a couple steps and stopped a few meters from his son who turned around and lifted the spear and when the old man took another step closer and fell on his knees the son thrust the spear into his chest with great force and pulled it back out."

Jonathan started. One of his legs moved from side to side and he turned toward Bill.

"And then it was all over, right? He was dead."

"Yes, he was dead. And he and his family were spared having to go through the prolonged ordeal of illness."

Bill recalled the humming of voices when the old man collapsed to the ground and the son who let out a scream and ran out of the tent and he described to Jonathan how the men then focused all their attention on the deceased. They smeared blood on their faces and became one with him in the same way they did with the reindeer blood during the autumn hunt. Whereupon they placed a hood on the deceased and walked around his corpse as they kicked it and growled like bears in order to chase evil spirits away.

"What was it like seeing a person die like that?" Jonathan asked in such a subdued voice that Bill could hardly hear it.

"I can't explain it," he began. "Well, it was like a dream had me in that tent and I didn't react until I sensed the smell of blood. I felt nausea coming up in my throat and I rushed out of the tent and ran through the snow and vomited until there was nothing left but bile."

"You could in a way say the son was forced to kill his own father, couldn't you?" Jonathan asked.

"I don't think he had much choice. His father had ordered him to do it." He paused. "I won't ever forget the look in his son's eyes when he approached his father with the spear."

"How will he ever get out over that?"

Bill nodded and he closed his eyes. After the seance in the tent he trampled amongst frost-covered larch trees that grew sporadically in an endless maze. He continued through the forest and at one point caught sight of a figure in the snow leaning against a tree, it was the son. Bill lowered himself next to him and they sat in silence as the rising sun cast shadows among the trees until Bill stood, pulling him up, pulling Jonathan up. They walked to the camp as Bill continued toward Leonid who was standing next to two men. They had toppled a reindeer onto its side and held it down as a third man stabbed it close to its heart with a spear so the animal didn't die right away but lay twitching. Its tremblings initiated the sleigh that would carry the deceased to the other world.

"What did they do with the dead man, did they bury him?

Bill walked beside Jonathan on the beach, stopped and took a firm grip on his arm.

"No, he was cremated. They prepared a bonfire at the top of the hill outside camp and were in a hurry to light it. When a person dies a channel's opened to the world for ancestors and those who are dead to go get the loved ones they long for. The channel won't close until you have gone through certain rituals and the deceased turned into ashes."

"So, they're afraid of the dead?"

"The reindeer people love and fear their dead. The way they see it, ancestors both provide life and take it away."

"I don't understand."

"In their consciousness, the dead continue to live in a parallel reality where they miss their loved ones and want them to die as quickly as possible so they can be reunited with them, something that has to happen before they themselves are born again into a new body in the old world."

"I like the idea of being reunited with those I love that are dead. Even if it's only for a moment."

Bill sensed Jonathan's smile encompassing him and he breathed more freely and deeply and the sun, the sun shone on them as they continued along the beach, until they crossed the cliffs, passed the airport and Jonathan walked one way and he the other.

The sky was now empty of clouds, Bill noticed, as he sauntered through town to the pier. The ferry had just left the bay and passengers were standing in a row along the railing looking back toward the island, as though they regretted having left. He sat on a bench on the pier, followed the ferry with his eyes until it could just as well have been a seagull rocking back and forth on the surface of the sea.

Bill had the feeling there was something good lying in wait. He couldn't remember the last time he had felt that way and it didn't really matter, anyway. The past was a mirage, a hodgepodge of complications, conditions, interpretations that triggered forth a sense of confusion and unrest within him.

Maybe there were lines and structures in his life that made sense if you looked at it retrospectively but right now he was unable to identify them. He closed his eyes and sensed the wind on his face, the songs of the waves, the cries of passing seagulls louder and softer in intensity and as he sat there everything that happened before his arrival to the island gathered into a deep, dark fog that shrank into a black ball, the eye of a needle, a particle that lifted itself from the top of his head and disappeared at the speed of light out into the universe.

A little while later he got back on his feet and walked toward town. He was going to meet Bear.

Taking Bear for a Walk

Bear appeared in the tall grass and came to greet him. Bill petted his muzzle, looked into his transparent jelly-like eyes that reflected his own face. He wondered whether the horse saw the same world he did and itself in it, the essence of stars, a particle in the universe which it was at one with? Bear shook his head rapidly, backed up a few steps and continued grazing. Morten came walking in tick-resistant rubber boots and asked Bill how his neck was.

"I consulted your stand-in and things are much better, also with my elbow."

The whites of Morten's eyes had a red tinge and his movements were heavy. At that moment the sun hit his face, revealing a net of fine wrinkles. His lips moved.

"Want to ride him?" he asked.

"I don't know. I think Bear is afraid of me. He might pick up my nervousness."

"He's definitely not afraid."

"I'd like to."

"Then take a little ride."

Bill nodded and Morten adjusted the saddle, helped him up and pulled him around on the fenced-in lawn.

"Now I'll let you try on your own."

"What if he starts galloping and throws me off?"

"He's as calm as ..."

"...his owner?" Bill asked.

"I can't claim that. Anyway, Bear is only calm during the day, at night, well, that's a different story, that's when his horns and wings start peeping forth."

Bill smiled and took the reins. The horse trotted along and stopped at an electric fence. He opened the gate to the road and rode toward town square, past the church, the picket fence to the parsonage. Mie was sitting on the footstep with her youngest child, her slightly older child lying on a blanket with a duvet and comic books, the oldest ones were playing badminton, she looked up. I don't think I'm ever sleeping with you again, he thought. She caught sight of him and came out to the road.

"Is he one of Morten's?"

"He saved my life and we became friends."

"That sounds dramatic."

"It was."

She pursed her lips and blinked, naked on the floor in front of the wood stove.

"Grab the opportunity," she immediately said.

"For what?"

"Happiness. Come to the services tomorrow."

"When I'm supposed to go to my friend's funeral?"

"That's not what I meant. We'll start mass in the morning and afterward there will be a formal ceremony in the chapel and in the church. Will you be there?"

Bill nodded and let Bear choose the direction they would continue riding in.

Felix arrived at the clinic holding hands with his aunt who was going in first. She pointed at a chair in the waiting room and gave him a magazine with comic strips. Barbara asked Felix whether he wanted anything to drink, got some juice and closed the door.

"My big sister wants you to come by," she said quickly.

"And she has no scruples?"

"When I told her about Felix she softened up."

"How is she doing now?"

"I can't describe. Horribly. I hope you'll have time to visit today?"

Barbara nodded.

"Write down her address and I'll go when my shift's over," she said, considering whether she ought to talk with Morten, but decided to see the ailing woman without being influenced by her medical records.

The aunt placed the paper on the table.

"I'd like to see Felix now. You can take his place in the waiting room."

The boy entered through the door and closed it carefully behind him. She pointed to the chair and he sat down.

"It's wonderful to see you again, Felix. How are you doing?"

"Good."

"Do you ever think about what happened when you fell in the water?"

He nodded.

"My mom says I should try to forget it."

"Can you?"

"I think about it when I have to go to sleep."

"Every night?"

He nodded again and Barbara took his hands and gently caressed them.

Then she got up and positioned herself in back of him, placed her hands on his shoulders and the moment he looked up and saw her she knew that a balance had been created that involved a male fetus in a steel dish one night eight years ago and a good deal of all the things that event had brought with it.

"I want you to know that it will pass. Suddenly you'll discover you haven't thought about it for several days until finally the experience will be like a small dot in the sky you won't even know what it is."

He nodded and she was caught in his clear blue eyes.

THE BUTTERFLY

When Barbara said goodbye to Felix and his aunt a couple more patients arrived, the removal of a verruca, blood pressure and prescription renewal, before she was done for the day. She needed air and trod into the darkness and found herself at the top of a small hill squinting against the sun when a butterfly landed in the flower garden and spread its white wings out towards the goldeness. She carefully went closer and sat in the sand. The tips of its wings had gray angular spots. It could have been the Real's Wood White that was missing in the seventh wooden box with its glass lid piled with other wooden boxes in the stock room where she stored her things.

She hadn't looked through them after her father's death. Then it took off, and Barbara followed from flower to flower until it allowed itself to be pulled up into the heights to disappear like time itself.

She found the house on her phone's GPS and slowly began to make her way there. The afternoon sun trembled about the branches of trees when she approached from the side of the desert and stopped at the dividing line. Foggy, blue light penetrated through windows on the ground floor. Barbara stepped in among pine trees, noticed the flickering TV screen and her own pulse whizzing through her ears. The woman was lying on her couch underneath a blanket and Jonathan was sitting next to her on a chair. He raised a glass to her lips, placed it back on the table, said something or other, her head moved, he stood and got something in the kitchen.

It felt wrong going in while Jonathan was there. Did he even know that she was coming? He disappeared once more and came back wearing a jacket and kissed his mother, the door shut, there was fidgeting in the bicycle shed and afterward she saw him biking down the road toward town. Barbara waited a moment before crossing the lawn, walking round the house and finally knocking on the door, opened it and and announced who she was but there was no response.

"It's the doctor," she repeated louder as she thoroughly wiped her feet on the door mat, stepped onto the red-brown tiles repeated in the hallway and in the living room, stopped at the door opening.

"I'm sorry for barging in like this," she said.

There was still no response from the couch. An ad for pills against pollen allergy filled the screen, she sat on the chair where Jonathan had been before. The woman had sunken cheeks and there was a stench of an unwashed human body in the room. She breathed slowly and her body experienced pain between moments of calmness. Barbara cleared her throat, placed her hand on her arm and squeezed lightly but the woman was in a distant layer of consciousness due to the medicine. Barbara felt her forehead, cold sweat, and for a few seconds she considered whether she should hospitalize her. There were plenty of signs indicating that might be the right thing to do, but a few gurgling sounds came from the woman's throat and she opened her eyes wide and stared straight ahead.

"I know who you are," she said practically inaudibly as it had been her last breath and stared with a blood-shot gaze in her sunken face.

Barbara started in surprise, making the chair fall with a bang, pulling a few newspapers with it. She quickly stood the chair upright and sank down in it again, and was just about to explain herself.

"The prodigal daughter has returned," the woman

immediately whispered, placing her hand on Barbara's cheek, it smelled of soil and rubbing alcohol.

"You were standing alone in the steam at the place where the lightning struck after the electrical discharge." She gasped for air. "You are looking for answers that don't exist and can therefore be pursued for a whole lifetime."

Her voice faded like the inescapable movement of twilight toward darkness. Barbara recognized Jonathan's eyes deep down in hers that trembled like butterfly wings in a poison glass.

"I am a doctor and I'm standing in for Morten. Your sister asked me to see you," she said.

The television gave off flickering images and voices that spoke all at once which Barbara tried to ignore.

"Morten means well, and so do my sisters," she whispered with a sudden sense of intimacy in her voice.

"People always mean well and want the best for others, but they make the mistake of seeing things from their own perspective."

"You're right. But as a doctor..."

"This has got to stop for the sake of my boy, Jonathan," she interrupted her. "Get me into a hospital, Barbara."

She let out a loud sigh and her hand slid down to the duvet and her eyes shut. Shortly afterward Barbara could tell by the way she was breathing that she was asleep.

She remained for a little while before going out to the hallway, shut the door behind, started making her way down a narrow, brick street with a view of the cleft of the sky between high walls, cloud formations floated across houses, the street sloped, grew narrower and ended at a shut door. Sounds came out of her mouth, somebody wrapped her in a cloth, placed on her warm breast and kissed her over and over. She stopped and looked around. The gravel road meandered through the area, soft branches hung across the road, a blackbird singing, some animal or other scraping and pecking close by, perhaps a squirrel keeping an eye on her? She floated among branches and landed on the summerhouse terrace, opened the door and walked into the entrance and when she removed her jacket she saw a white butterfly sitting on the back of it with its wings folded. Barbara placed the jacket on the chair on the terrace and went to the kitchen and put up some water for coffee. When she returned it was gone.

A Visit from the Poet

A bell rang. Barbara looked up from the sunny spot in front of the house. Jonathan jumped off his bike and pulled it the last part of the way.

"I'm sorry for dropping by like this but you said ..."

"Did you bring the poems?"

He tapped his shoulder bag.

"And sorry for sweating, I took a long bike ride before shopping for dinner."

"What's in the bags?"

"I brought some food with me, I get a discount at the supermarket."

They sat at table with tapas on ceramic plates in a narrow passage between picturesque buildings with narrow balconies, fried octopus arms, shrimps in garlic, flutes with paté, grilled squash, red wine. Afterward Barbara couldn't recall what they had talked about, the temperature went down, and twilight settled like a cool membrane across the harbor, she blew out the candles and carried the plates and utensils into the kitchen. The house warmed by the sun and she opened the window, leaned toward the stars, heard someone humming and observed Jonathan through the window to the bathroom. He was soaping himself underneath the shower, letting water dribble down his body and then stood in front of her in the living room, trees swaying outside, placed his hand on her arm, pulled her through the the door to the closest room.

"How about a drink?" she asked, feeling his lips.

They were lying with their faces toward each other on the narrow bed when the sky exploded in moonlight and the shivers moved down her back.

Later Jonathan took out his mobile phone and read a poem out loud for her:

"Together with you my doubt burns to dust, making my words fall into completed patterns."

"I'm happy to hear that," she said, "and couldn't help laughing.

He didn't know the extent to which she had lost her way, she was roaming about in the chaos she had created, the grip of fogginess from which she couldn't escape, the mud she was stuck in. Jonathan's finger slid down the cell phone and he continued reading:

"I dreamed all people lived eternally, could travel unhindered throughout the universe and settle exactly where they wished. Gender didn't exist. A human was a human."

Barbara led his hand to her mouth and kissed it, sank back into the bed. The blessed bell-rain of the wind in the childhood birch trees embraced her and she registered millennia of variations on her own life.

"In the dreams, in the poems, the beats of my heart are synchronous with that of the universe," he continued and nodded toward piles of papers he had placed on the table. "And you'll find over one hundred pages with words, if you have the energy for it."

Barbara remembered she had arrived at the island with a momentary loud, shrill sound in her ears. There could have been concrete, physiological explanations for that but she had also read somewhere it was a sign that a person's state of consciousness was ascending, but she couldn't take it seriously. At any rate, the sound followed her tiredlessly like a wolf hunting its prey. Even though she ran fast, trying to keep it at bay, it got closer to her, snapped at her fluttering clothes. While she was lying there in the bed she noticed that the sound had disappeared and her mind was silent. Jonathan smiled in his sleep, she caressed his hair, his breathing grew heavier, she kissed his forehead.

Her grandmother said, "You are a dear, Barbara." You never grew too old for that, they stood on the kitchen floor and embraced one another, Barbara inhaled the scent of her in her lungs.

Her face was furrowed, her hair concealed underneath her scarf, her eyes shaped like almonds, full of insight. They sat on the bench by the stream at the bottom of the yard lost in their thoughts staring across the water which was pulled by the current, changed colors and structure according to the sun's position and movement of the clouds.

When morning came she gently disengaged from Jonathan's arms and took a bath. She could almost, but only almost, have been his mother and when she stood in front of him with her towel wrapped around her body he was awake and looking at her as though saying: You should do what you feel is right and not what the world expects of you.

"Are we seeing each other again?" he asked.

Barbara searched for a way to tell him that late in the afternoon, right before he came, she had made a call to get his mother hospitalized.

"You don't have to decide now," he continued.

She walked over to him and felt his hands on her

body, kissed his ear, wanted to say there are questions that are meaningless to find the answer to if he didn't want to end up a slave to fear.

"Your mother..." she began.

"Good you mentioned it, I need to get back and see to her."

"She was hospitalized this morning. I spoke with her yesterday and she asked me to make sure she got hospitalized."

Jonathan jumped from the couch and fetched his shoes, he couldn't untie his shoelaces and she helped him.

"Why didn't you tell me until now?"

"Morten just notified me the ambulance had picked her up."

"Did Morten inform you?"

Jonathan stopped in the middle of his tracks, turned toward her as though he was about to say something, but regretted it.

"I'll have to go, but we'll see each other again," he then said, quickly kissed her and before she had a chance to respond he rushed out the door, shook the dew drops off the bicycle and disappeared among the trees.

Bill entered the chapel and found a chair by the entrance. It smelled of tar and moisture in the brick building which was a good six meters on one side and eight on the other. Crosswise, there lay deeply slashed beams of one and a half meters between them and invited one to crawl up to them to train one's balancing skills or take a few arm lifts just to prove it was still possible. Jonas's oldest son, around twenty, was swaying over the stone floor in front of the coffin which was decorated with purple flowers, his hands at the ends of his sleeves moved like independent creatures. His little brother sat frozen, looking straight ahead, his eyes full of tears. Aside from their confirmations, Bill hadn't seen the boys since they were little because whenever he and Jonas met it was without their families, always just them alone.

Alone on one-day excursions around lakes and forests. Alone on roller skis along deserted roads in the provinces. Alone in rented canoes meandering rivers. Alone at restaurants, bars, night clubs. Alone at the hot dog stand at four o'clock in the morning. Alone on the island in week 25. He would never forget that day. Jonas called and said there was something wrong with his body. The routine blood tests had shown signs of disease even though he couldn't feel anything and he had to immediately be scanned. From one moment to the next he was categorized as sick and started treatments and he was overwhelmed by the side effects and nothing was as before except for brief moments where there seemed to be flashes of normalcy.

That wasn't how things were supposed to have turned out. They were supposed to have gotten older and older until they had gotten ancient, taking small walks together along the water and in the forest talking about the past and things they still dreamed about, together in one another's company, as always, because it was good. Now Jonas was gone and there was nothing to understand, the world missed him, Bill missed him. If Leonid had been here he would have consolingly said it wasn't the end forever, that they would meet again, that Jonas was somewhere else waiting for him there.

Perhaps that really was how things worked, but did that depend on deep, inner knowledge?

Bill remembered something Jonas had said during one of his first hospitalizations:

"Why cling to religion? Instead of facing the reality that death shuts down everything, and believe in life while you are still alive instead?"

Bill couldn't remember what he had answered. Now he registered something moving above him and caught sight of a raven scraping leaves on the roof window of the chapel, its eyes beaming through the room as Jonas's son bent forward and kissed the coffin. The body heat from the living had chased the deathly coldness away and Bill wiped the sweat from his hair line with a finger, heard Jonas's voice say the whole thing was so strange, as though all periods of time merged together into one present and he was standing in the middle of it and didn't know where to go. The blue-white semi-light from the window hit Jonas's bed and he raised his hand into the light and absorbed it until his body was filled to the brim and when he took Bill's hand in his, he also became a part of the light and they got up and slid into the crowd that walked behind the coffin.

"There are days when the rain hits you like little sour drops."

Jonas's favorite song had started playing on the stereo. "And the whole world leans so far down that the only way is up."

Bill could no longer hold back tears, stared fixedly down at the floor, concentrated on his balance, avoided the gaze of others. The hearse stood ready, the coffin pushed into place, and the undertaker in his suit bowed deeply as the song faded away inside the chapel.

Bill positioned himself close to a gray-bearded man, Jonas's big brother, whom he knew from childhood and had since seen at family get-togethers but hadn't spoken to for decades and tried to catch his gaze to no avail. The right thing to do would be to give his condolences.

"I refuse to enter the church," Jonas' brother said at that very moment, lit a cigarette and took a big drag.

Bill caught fragments of the sentence addressed to an older woman. Something about God being a cloak for humanity, a toxic cocktail of ineffective prayers and a disclaimer of responsibility.

Bill suppressed a smile, followed the crowd toward the church. Mie bid everyone welcome at a massive wooden door, her cool hand in his, he couldn't read her. He took a seat furthest back, the sound of shoes clicking against stone covered floors with inscriptions, priests, years, the names of wealthy individuals who had contributed to salvation and immortality. The black priest's robe made its way to the altar.

Mie turned around and started speaking, "the triumph of the present moment" were words he registered in the stream of words that were to soothe their pain, rinse away their fear, instill hope, the surrender to the knowledge of their inner being, hand in hand with God. The priest's robe heaved up and down, dancing like a balloon held by the flow of heat by gas flames that caressed her and she made the sign of the cross when he penetrated her and remained there. He felt her warm breath on his cheek, the voices of the choir singers resounded back from walls and ceilings, drilled into the brain and hurled toward the cranium, as you would hurl yourself with all your might at a blockaded door in a burning house. He ordered the unpleasantness to go away whereupon it rose, exploded like lit gunpowder under fresco paintings, sprinkling sparks down across the participants.

Bill joined the funeral wake in the meeting house, the sons sat next to each other at the longest of the tables. Mie across from them. He approached them.

"I don't know if you remember me." He sensed the lump in his throat, cleared it.

They looked at him, somewhat confused.

"I clearly remember. But it's a long time ago we last saw each other. Your father was a really good friend of mine."

"I recognize you. You're Bill, right?" said the big brother who had eulogized at the coffin. "You were the one Father went on vacation with in week 25."

Bill nodded.

"Exactly. I just wanted to say I feel so sad for you, for all of us.

They nodded simultaneously, said nothing and Bill was reminded of his own son whom he hadn't seen in ages and suddenly missed.

"I don't want to disturb you any more. Maybe we'll talk a little later."

Bill quickly placed a hand on their shoulders, met Mie's gaze and looked for a table. He recognized several of the faces, Jonas's aunt and uncle sat silently, looking straight ahead, a couple of cousins chattering away and laughing, looking right through him. Bill considered walking over to them but it didn't seem right that he, a stranger whom they had danced with on a wedding night ages ago, would interrupt their conversation and stand there trying to find something to talk about so he continued in the direction of the draught beers and the snack bowls which were already half empty. There were people gathered around all the tables except for one by the end wall where Bill sat with his draught beer and watched his son walk amongst the trees in the darkness of his mind without looking back. The chunk of Chorizo grew in his mouth and new refreshments were placed on the buffet, smoked Greenland halibut with mustard sauce, but Bill couldn't get another bite down.

He was sitting under a gold-framed painting of grazing cows in a hilly landscape, in the background a mill towered, dizzy, his stomach sloshing around, one of the sons looked like Jonas when he was young, the other different, blonde, blue-eyes, small nose. Mie smiled at him when he glided across the room and stepped outside. The air was heavy with humidity, it was windy, his legs led him to the cemetery, the sky opened, the rain hit his face, rinsed away a sense of dizziness, gusts of wind made oak trees creak, flowers from the chapel were lying at the foot of one them. Death is life longing for the formless world of light.

He shook off the thought, trembled from cold, the

clouds black, whispering trees, a mush of fog lingered above the cemetery, his legs moved, the rest of his body followed out to the street in direction of the wilderness.

He could have continued forever, that was what he could have done, from one world to the next and to the next and that was what he did until he pulled the duvet up to his neck and let the back of his neck sink through layers of down until it hit the mattress, the sleeping pad, the sound of the zipper, the canvas of the tent being pushed aside and Jonas's smiling face appearing. He was holding two bottles of beer in his hand, clinked them together and said:

"A last one by the bonfire before we settle down for the night, what do you say?"

The Good Life

Barbara caught sight of Bill in front of the medical health center where he stood looking at the sign with opening hours when she suddenly twisted her ankle, screamed louder than expected and hit the asphalt hard. Bill came running and pulled her up by her arm, she sensed his scent.

"Damn, and that's not the first time. Could you help me inside?"

She felt his decisiveness, the muscles in his arm when she grabbed a hold of it. He supported her up the four steps of stone stairs and she limped on one leg through the waiting room, opened the door to the clinic, collapsed in the chair and waited for her pulse to stabilize.

"Come on in," she shouted shortly afterward.

She was now sitting with her back to the writing desk, her foot on the book shelf, the reference books pushed to the side, the ankle was already swollen.

"Being at work is going to be challenging today," she said, extending her arms.

"Well, there's no escaping having to put some ice on

the swelling. Can I get you to check the ice box in the kitchen?"

Bill returned with an ice bag and placed it on her ankle. Most of the red on her toe nail had peeled off and her foot resembled marble or rather pig's skin and there were stripes from her stocking. She cursed under her breath.

"I've tried the same thing, the worst thing was the long-term side effects, I kept twisting my ankle for years afterward because the tendon had gotten slack, I kept falling on sidewalks, bicycle paths, in pedestrian crossings before it finally subsided." He hesitated. "But that doesn't necessarily mean the same thing will happen to you."

Bill looked at her back and they both started to laugh.

"Do you live close by?" he asked.

"Almost a kilometer away."

"Is there anyone who can help you? Morten, maybe?"

"He's busy with his horses, I'll have to stay a few hours, but there might not be any patients."

"Can I be your assistant, then? I could also help you get home afterward."

"That's kind of you, but it won't be necessary," she said without meaning it.

"I've got nothing else to do."

She practically turned her head out of joint and looked at him with a smile, her hands folded instinctively in her lap, clinging to one another. A door opened and some fidgeting could be heard in the waiting room.

"There are customers," said Bill.

He looked at her quizzically.

"Yes, thank you, please accompany me home when I'm done here."

She removed the ice pack, lifted her leg down from the book shelf and placed it under the writing desk. There were butterflies in her stomach and the feeling spread to her chest.

"See you, then, and I'll be fine," she said.

*

Barbara shut the door behind her. She had wrapped her foot in an elastic bandage and used Bill as support. The sun was shining on their backs and followed their shared shadow that glided across the street.

At long last they approached the house behind

the tall pine trees and walked along the springy trail with red ants darting along carrying needles and tiny branches between their jaws, the ocean was roaring, a squirrel observed them vigilantly. Bill helped her inside, said something about the papers spread across the dining room table and she collapsed into the armchair and answered she wasn't the writer, she was just reading poems for someone she knew. She had thought of Jonathan continually throughout the day and had been about to call him to ask about his mother but instead she contacted the hospital and was told she was in a coma. Out from the kitchen Bill asked if he should make dinner for her, there was squash, red peppers, onions, eggs as part of the service pack, and she laughed and said what she needed was some wine but if he would make an omelet he'd have to eat it with her and they were going to sit outside. Bill opened a bottle and poured wine into their glasses, placed the plates on the terrace table upon which the sun was shining through the trees, helped her into her chair, the wind had died down. He lit a cigarette.

"I started again after my divorce, I'll soon stop again," he said apologetically.

"Of course you will. Can I have one?"

He lit one for her and she inhaled the smoke down into her lungs and started coughing. He handed her the glass.

"Maybe you just shouldn't start?" he said, laughing.

"You mean, I ought to listen to my body's signals?"

"Isn't that what you're supposed to do?" There was still a big smile on his face.

"In most situations, yes."

"When shouldn't one listen, then?"

"There can be moments where the brain says one thing and the heart another."

"Who'll win then?"

"There are no rules for that." They sat in silence for a short while before she said:

"So, you're also divorced?"

"We were together fifteen years before she moved on to fresh pastures."

"Do you have children?"

"I have an adult son from a previous marriage. We didn't have any together. How about you?"

"It's almost the same story, minus the son."

She started coughing again.

"I haven't smoked since my student days."

"A smoking medical student," he said.

"At that time I was studying physics."

She described her failed dream of becoming a physicist and exposing areas that hadn't been described before and for which regularities had not yet been established, a language one could lean on.

"But I quickly understood the extent of my naïveté," she said. "Having success in that world presupposes intellectual acknowledgment of a caliber I can only dream about so I switched to medicine, chose a path where I photograph the visible world instead of striving to cover invisible meanings, layer upon layer, something that can move us humans. I became an ordinary general practitioner."

"There's no shame in admitting one isn't a genius and then getting the best out of it," he said.

Barbara laughed out loud.

"Anyway, what are you doing here on the island, Bill?"

He explained that after his journey and the divorce he had taken leave from university.

"In order to recover?"

"I used that as an explanation but it's more accurate

to say I hope to digest all sorts of things and then see what will come out if it. My thought was to go to one of the places on the planet where I felt my best. First goal was to visit my friend, Jonas."

"Does he live on the island?"

"He died the other day at the new hospice out at the camping site."

"I'm sorry to hear."

"Yes, hard to understand we won't ever see each other again." He hesitated. "It's a bit like one's life being sucked from meaning."

"It might end that way for all of us, that there's no more meaning."

"I hope not."

She caught his gaze and held it for a few seconds until he looked away.

"Me too."

"After my latest journey and after I've become single I caught sight of the fact my life in many ways has been controlled by something others expected of me, by my own unrealistic goals which I tried to live up to. The one common denominator being I worked against that which I felt is my essence. And that's something I want to stop doing."

"Your essence?"

A vertical wrinkle appeared between his eyes.

"I know it sounds stupid and it may not really cover it, but what I really mean is, apropos what you said before, in many ways I followed my brain and have gone against my heart."

"I can't claim to know what my essence is," she said. "But I think I ended up in a similar trap and perhaps I also came to the island in order to try to escape that essence. Imagine if you could disengage your own and others' expectations about something specific having to happen which in reality isn't good for one?"

"Yes, and imagine if you could create so much peace within yourself you weren't in doubt as to when it was right to say yes or no?"

They looked at each other and he chuckled faintly. "Should I make some food?"

"If you want to. We could also order out?"

"No, that's alright, I don't mind doing it," he said and went inside.

Barbara could hear him fidgeting in the kitchen and she closed her eyes, sensed her body's movement toward a state of calm. When he served the omelet the setting sun trembled amongst the trees. They ate and talked about her medical practice and he about his travels in the wilderness and gradually they moved back in time.

"And you also came here to the island as a child, then?" Bill asked, placing his utensils down.

She nodded.

"For me there is, on the one hand, a rosy, innocent childhood happiness and a big ocean of sorrow tied up with this place," she said.

"Why sorrow?"

A bell rang, a young man threw his bike on the grass, half ran, stopped abruptly.

"Jonathan?" she asked. "This is Bill, he..."

"Hi, Jonathan," Bill interrupted. "We met each other the other day," he said to Barbara.

"I ... I just wanted to get my manuscript."

"Of course, it's on the dining room table, but I'm not done reading it," she said.

"I visited my mother at the hospital. She's in a respirator," he said when he came out with the papers.

"Isn't that also the best thing?" Barbara asked.

An indefinable expression came over his face and he nodded and quickly went to his bike.

"I'll call you," she shouted to Jonathan's back.

At that moment he stopped on his bike and turned toward them with a big smile.

"I just want to say you two look very well together."

Before they had a chance to respond he disappeared through the trees and Barbara didn't know what to say except it was getting cold and then they went inside. Bill filled the dishwasher and started it and sat next to her in the couch.

"You must be tired," he said. "And I had better get home."

"My foot's already beginning to feel better. I don't think the sprain was so bad after all."

She hesitated and wanted him to stay.

"Isn't there another bottle?" she asked.

He got it and poured some wine into glasses while she racked her brain to come up with something that would make him stay."

"The multiverse," she exclaimed "That was what interested me while studying physics"

"The multiverse?"

"If two universes move in the exact same quantum state then they're identical which means there are universes fully or almost identical to ours."

She caught his gaze and it seemed as though he was interested. Perhaps there had been a correlation between that and the indigenous people he had been researching. He nodded, at any rate, which she interpreted as a sign to go on:

"The universes are more or less identical to ours, situated close, but little by little they develop and become increasingly different, the distance between them and us continues to grow."

"That sounds as though you believe it?" he said.

"It's based on firmly established knowledge. Research has proven there are deviations from normal gravity which according to leading specialists, indicate there are parallel universes less than 10 centimeters from our own."

She observed a drop of sweat that left Bill's forehead and moved down his cheek.

"The reindeer people with whom I lived in the wilderness," he immediately said, "operated with parallel universes as well, and they must at all costs be kept separate. The people who have died in this world and live in another place miss their loved ones whom they can no longer be with here, terribly and vice versa.

According to their train of thought it's possible to cross the boundary between worlds and see loved ones again, but the price is a bloody and daunting chaos. But what would a physicist say to the idea that one's body or perhaps consciousness can exist in several universes at the same time?"

"They'd frown upon that, but the question is also whether trying to fathom something which our limited brains can't fathom is, in fact, an impossible task?"

She fixed Bill's gaze and then let go. She felt like kissing him, but didn't know how to get to where it would feel natural. Bill smiled. What if he didn't feel the same way? He slowly got up.

"Thank you for a wonderful evening," he began.

Her hand was on the armrest of the couch and he patted it lightly like an old aunt might have done.

"You too. Thank you for transporting me safely home and cooking dinner for me. It tasted really good."

"We'll probably run into each other again, won't we?" Bill asked when he was standing in the door, a nerve quivered on his forehead, the darkness seemed to be pulling at him.

"I probably won't be going anywhere far the next couple of days, but yes."

She limped over to him and placed her hand on his hip as though she were supporting herself on him.

He didn't seem to know what to say, either, and then he started telling her about an article he had once written which took its point of departure in the story of an author who experienced synchronicity at full blast. The author had in their youth eaten plum pudding with a male acquaintance at a restaurant. The man appeared at the restaurant at intervals of decades at a time and ordered plum pudding the same exact few times that the author revisited the place with the same purpose. She didn't have the heart to tell him she already knew the story, pressed against his hip, he seemed as solid as a rock and she felt like sliding over and feeling his arms around her.

"That was mere coincidence," she said to provoke him a little and trigger a reaction that would open a crack she could penetrate.

"Perhaps it was," said Bill. "But the point is meaning's created because everything in the universe is connected ."

When she let go of his hip he took her hand and held it in his. She yawned loudly.

"I'm sorry," she blurted, laughing a little. "It's been a long day."

"Maybe you'd like to go for a hike up to the lighthouse when your foot's recovered?"

She felt her heart racing.

"That would be nice, I haven't seen seals since I was a child."

"We'll text each other about it then?"

She pulled him to her and they stood holding each other for a couple seconds before she kissed his cheek, gently pushed him out the door and watched as he disappeared into the darkness.

The Moment of the Solar Eclipse

The following morning Barbara suddenly remembered the bag of yarn in the luggage, the knitting needles were there, the directions for knitting a sweater, blue with red patterns on the chest, not so complicated, but it called for thin pins and it would take time. Jonathan might like it, or Bill, and then Jonathan called.

"We distance ourselves from eternity in order to long for reconnection," he said without introducing himself.

"Hi Jonathan. I'm mostly preoccupied with the present," Barbara switched to listening-in mode and placed the phone on the table. The elastic bandage was feeling too tight and she took it off. When will you be able to go out to the lighthouse, little foot?

"I wrote this to my mother," he continued, "When during a solar eclipse moment you walked into the forest without looking back, I pulled your farewell deep into my lungs and pronounced the words, 'I love you. 'What do you think?"

"It's very fine. Have you read it aloud to her?"

"Not yet. I'm sitting on the ferry and on my way to the hospital."

Barbara registered the noise of wind, the humming of a ship's engine, she continued knitting, had cast on the stitches and had started on the back part when the telephone rang, it was very straightforward, images wound around one another, hazy figures floated by. Now she was roaming down the usual dark street when the rays of sun hit her face and connected everything in non-integer beauty, rain poured down the window panes, her thoughts were gusts of wind, light dawned, the grass newly-rinsed green, and there were butterflies everywhere.

"What would love say if it could speak?" Jonathan asked.

She let the knitting things fall to her lap.

"How long do you think my mom has left?" he continued.

"It's hard to say but her time's coming. It could be today, tomorrow, in a week."

"Thank you, Barbara."

They were cut off and she slid back into the couch and closed her eyes.

A little while later she was standing by the open door registering the waves that reached across the beach, pulling the pebbles, pine trees swayed in the wind, gulls shouting Jonathan's name.

JONATHAN

Jonathan sat by his mother's side holding her hand. The respirator breathing for her. Now he got up, whispered something in her ear and turned off the machine. He lay on the bed and held her, lifted himself above the landscape with which he was familiar and caught sight of a slender man wearing a reindeer outfit. Jonathan followed the man who walked through the wilderness in rapid strides.

On a bed of stone, at the top of the tallest sand dune, her body lay under the sky for all to see. The man stopped in his tracks, let out a growl and lifted the knife, stuck it into her stomach and led it up to her bottom rib. He turned the cut surfaces inside out and pulled out her intestines. Her stomach, liver, kidneys. The interconnected organ system lay there steaming as her blood formed a blubbering pool in a depression in the sand. The knife continued its wanderings and with all the might he could muster in his sinewy arms and shoulders, he opened her ribcage and tore out her lungs and heart. He cut along the edge of her bone as when one fillets a fish and pulled the meat from her torso and face and continued with the hips, thighs, and lower legs. Then he carefully turned her on her stomach and removed the remaining flesh from her feet, legs, thighs, back and back of her neck and head until her bloody skeleton lay bare in all its perfection. Then he removed the last residuals of flesh from bone, wiped her fingers and took the drum he'd fastened on her back and started tapping it with his hand. First slowly then faster as the words floated from him and encompassed the desert, the island, the ocean, the planet, the universe.

*You, raven woman with the long legs.
You dance to my song, dance to my song
You, raven woman dance to my song among the trees
    and down at the bog
You dance to my song in the water
and in the heathers
You dance to my song
On the steep slope and
 the fertile meadow
You dance to my song
You, raven woman with the long legs
You dance to my song, dance to my song
You, raven woman, dance to my song.

Now What Now

Bill and Barbara walked side by side along the gravel road that led to the desert where was still ground mist among sporadic hills and cold steam penetrated one's clothes. Bill felt his vision was as clear as it had been in youth and Barbara let herself be rocked back and forth by the distant rumbling sea. I'm not going to keep the conversation going, we're just going to wander along here, Bill thought, and Barbara said immediately afterward,

"It's a little funny calling a slightly hilly landscape with overgrown dunes like this a desert."

She pulverized a moss plant between her fingers and watched the wind carry the powder away.

"More sand than soil here. I hope it's not too hard on your foot."

"Or for the rest of me." She laughed briefly. "My sensitive, spirited ex husband once said when I don't sense the pulse of love I become very hard on myself."

Bill nodded and was about to say something when she gave him a careful nudge on his shoulder.

"You don't want to talk about your ex-husband?" he asked.

"No." She hesitated for a moment.

"But I have since considered the fact that his statement has a negative side for me. I probably have an internal nervousness for slipping up and therefore tend to go out of my way to show my nicest most predictable side as opposed to the less appropriate side. No frustration, rage, sorrow or whatever else may disappoint others so they might loathe me, talk behind my back, which blocks out whatever sort of love pulse there may be."

"So you're never completely yourself?"

"Whoever that is, as we spoke about the other day."

Bill thought about the last time they'd seen each other, when she shut the door behind him and he walked through trees toward the road, stopped, the light from the windows of the house, Barbara in the armchair and the forest alive, the trees had feelings, thought about things, missed those who'd disappeared, looked forward to seeing them again when they themselves fell for the storm or time, when there were no more branches left, the trunk dried, cracked, settled in the bottom of the forest, opened itself to insects and larvae who dug tunnels, found food, shelter from the cold, summer rain.

He had leaned against a young tree that wasn't as tall as the neighboring trees, narrow trunk, resilient without moss or gnarls. Branches created clever patterns and veins against the moonlit sky and he'd been thinking to himself she deserved someone better and then she probably wasn't interested in him at all.

Barbara looked at Bill who was walking a little ways ahead, she felt like jumping onto his back and letting him carry her but they didn't know each other that well.

They walked a long time without saying anything.

"Are you with me?" Bill asked without looking back.

"The sand's actually as heavy as a desert here."

He turned toward her. She was standing with arms crossed and deliberately defiant and he couldn't help smiling.

"Do you need a break?"

He pointed at her foot and she nodded, sat down in sand. Little foot, please pull yourself together. Bill was just about to ask whether they should just turn around and go back, eat lunch by the harbor maybe, he had seen a restaurant had just opened.

She thought there was something lost yet at the same time incomprehensible and lovable about him, plus something firmly established, the iron ball in the center of the earth, he made her feel all at once insecure and safe as had he been equipped with tentacles that penetrated her brain and created chaos and then order. She looked at his hand hanging in the air in front of her, chocolate, she took a piece, a steel cup caught the sun.

"We're about halfway to the lighthouse," said Bill.

He felt like telling her in his experience the things one wanted to forget tended to grow within, while the things we wanted to remember disappeared, but didn't remember why it was relevant, and instead extended his cup and they touched cups.

Barbara sipped the steaming tea and let chocolate melt in her mouth and when she caught sight of a cloud formation, a ladder between heaven and earth, it hit her as it had done again and again after she'd become single, that the bluntedness that pulsed through her kin would stop with her. She didn't want to see her children, if she ever got any, as a continuation of herself, her frustrations were not to play out through children who would have to manage well in life, not for their sake but for her own.

She inquired about Bill's upbringing.

"There isn't much to tell. My parents were just as predictable as other bourgeois families in the suburbs, money in their bank accounts, furnished homes in the usual classic way so as not to step out of line. My mother dressed my father in his finest when they went to opera, at home in living rooms they'd relax with cigarettes, sip whiskey, cheap vermouth. As though the whole thing had to be gotten over with."

"What?"

"The whole thing. What about yours?"

"My mother..." she hesitated. "Not to mention my stepfather. I have very little good to say about them."

Her stepfather looked at her with his eyes situated too close to one another, eyebrows tangled with coarse hair that stuck out in all directions, gray like the sporadic residuals of patches of hair on his head, stomach protruding, shirt several numbers too big for the rest of his upper body with narrow shoulders, thin arms that ended in small hands with short, fat fingers. Her mother, the ice queen, as Barbara's friends used to call her, would take love and affection with her to the grave, the only thing she'd leave behind would be an icy haze of narcissism best to avoid inhaling at all costs.

"My biological father, on the other hand..."

Barbara paused again, the wind caught her hair, she remembered the trees reflected in her father's pupils, he kissed her on the cheek, butterflies floated in slow-motion above her, clouds tumbled by like oxen across a plain. In the forest floor cycles played out, the brook meandered through a green landscape, a boat in dark water, her father stretched out on his back with eyes closed, drifted with the current that swirled on its surface, a lost shadow.

"Yes?" said Bill, looking at her.

"Yes, what?"

"Your biological father. Did you have a good relationship with him?" She sensed herself nodding.

"He died many years ago. We went on butterfly excursions, that's what I remember the best. He collected them and I thought I was going to acquire his interest when he died, but I couldn't get myself to kill them. It seemed meaningless to me to kill such a beautiful little creature and then place its dead body in a glass case, although that is pretty hypocritical considering all the animals that have suffered on my behalf just to fill my stomach."

"Is your mother still living?"

"Yes, alive and well. Full of life, destructive life, that is. Which reminds me of a dream I had the other day."

Whereupon she looked like a lost little girl.

"In the dream I lived with a bony woman in her 70's with a white-haired perm, red lips, I on the ground floor of a house and she on the second. She was clearly upset when she came down for breakfast in the common kitchen. 'Do you realize they've moved the house?' she asked.

When I contradicted her, her icy hand grabbed hold of my neck and squeezed so hard I couldn't breathe. I was paralyzed a few seconds and let her choke me before I collected myself and removed her hand. She extended her arms and apologized, rubbed her thighs, said that during the course of the night she had received visitors to her room, various creatures from distant planets, including a little elf-looking thing that resembled 'you quite a bit!' she screamed, pointing her finger in my direction. Her voice grew calm when she said the elf-creature confided to her something terrible had happened when she'd been conceived. Her father infested his semen with chemical oils so it went without saying she had turned out to be scum.

'He deserved the knife I drilled into his heart,' she hissed, hammering her fist into the table and making the plates and coffee cups jump.

'But now you get to see my back,' she continued, walking in rapid strides to the door and crossing the terrace.

I followed and saw her passing the street, reaching the beach, plodding into waves just before her head disappeared. She turned and shouted, 'See you in the country behind the ocean!'

It wasn't until then I realized she was my mother."

Barbara turned to Bill and took his hand. Her fingers cold and the coldness made hairs on his arm stand up.

"Right now I have the feeling everything I have believed has been a lie," she said, looking down at the sand.

*

Bill took the last steps toward the lighthouse, turned toward Barbara lagging behind, she sensed it was important for him to get there first, he tapped on the sun-baked cement column.

"Congratulations," she said and stopped in front of him, closer and closer with little, shuffling footsteps.

He was half a head taller. Her eyes were like the clear and frosty sky right after sunset, now she pursed her lips, closed her eyes, he moved his face the last few centimeters and kissed her. She felt his soft lips against hers, opened one of her eyes halfway, the sun and white clouds dancing round it, seals called and they disengaged from their embrace and walked to the water and took out their lunch packs. He noticed the sound of a distant engine and caught sight of a helicopter far off above the water.

They watched seals playing for a while before she said,

"One ought to become wiser about oneself the longer one lives, but the older I get the less I understand." Bill didn't answer immediately, but then said hesitantly,

"Perhaps because the world around us is changing so fast. Flightiness trumps predictability, curiosity drowned in unrest..."

"...and all that's left is eternal slavery, exhausted bodies and burned out minds?"

"Exactly," he said.

Barbara smiled inwardly and said,

"It's hard being alive."

"Are you being ironic?"

"No."

"And humanity will annihilate itself in this way," he said, though he himself could hear that the pitch of his voice had become increasingly dramatic. "But perhaps we should put insolvable problems to rest and just enjoy this?"

He got up and extended his arms, and she nodded and followed, put her hand in his back pocket and walked through the sun and the ocean and the clouds and he kissed her without hesitating which she wanted, for she received his kiss and kissed him back, and tapped his behind, found his hand and the heat from his body swept up through her as they swung their new shared body part back and forth, and he sensed a deeply stored feeling of joy growing from the airless darkness and gasp for breath.

They approached the remains of a dead seal by the edge of the water, surrounded by seagulls that squeaked and fought over bloody shreds on the ribs and then took off as a single flock as though someone had ordered them to do so, floated in circles in upward moving air currents. Just being alive, holding your hand, he thought, and at that moment she started running while swinging her arms like mill wheels.

Watch out for your foot, he was about to shout, when she stumbled and landed hard in the sand.

Barbara immediately knew this time it was serious, not just a sprain, and it hurt so much she started to cry when he helped her and she told him to call Morten immediately, he'd have to arrange for her to get picked up. She heard the telephone getting connected to the answering machine and Bill leaving a message.

"I'll have to carry you, then," he said. "How much do you weigh?"

"Too much, according to my sporty ex-husband," she moaned.

Bill moved his back pack to the front of his body, kneeled and pulled her onto his back so that she was able to rest her thighs against his hips, and started walking. She wasn't exactly light and he was an astronaut wearing a space suit. Barbara's arms wrapped around his neck and it sounded as though he had difficulty breathing, she really ought to lose a little weight, his footsteps grew slower and slower, he huffed and puffed, didn't complain, but his strength gave way and he carefully lowered her onto the sand.

Bill left her as he tried to locate a more or less sheltered depression in the dunes, put out the blanket, went to Barbara and carried her across the dunes and placed her in such a way that her foot could rest in an elevated position, her foot already warm, her pulse pounding beneath the flesh.

"I wonder when Morten will listen to his answering machine?" she said shortly afterward.

"It could be hours if he's out with the horses. If we call 911 a helicopter will come and pick you up."

"No, no, not for a broken foot. Helicopters are used for traffic accidents and that sort of thing. Morten will be sure to find a solution."

Bill considered the possibilities. It would get chilly once the darkness settled. He could walk 6-7 kilometers back to town and get help.

"You're not leaving me here all alone," she said, as though she could read his mind.

"No, of course not. Are you cold?"

"A little, perhaps."

He handed her the shirt from the backpack and she put it on underneath her windbreaker. It smelled of wool with an added scent of him, and she started creating a list in her mind of essential oils that combined would approach that particular scent but gave it up. Bill looked at her as she lay on the blanket, her gaze toward the sky and her lips moved imperceptibly as though she were chanting a silent prayer.

Her long legs disappeared underneath the jacket, one of her hands pulled him and he allowed himself to slide next to her, sand crunching between his teeth, she pressed her head underneath his chin, her hair smelled of ocean and salt and he maneuvered himself around until they lay cheek to cheek.

"You're scratching me a little," she whispered and their noses touched. "But that's okay, it's nice."

They breathed inaudibly and Barbara was thinking she wanted to kiss him, and was wondering what he was thinking.

"Who knows how long we're going to be here. I'd better make a bonfire," he said immediately.

"The wilderness man in action," she said, smiling.

Bill kissed her nose, went out to the desert and returned with his arms full of twigs, roots, and small branches as the twilight crept behind him among dunes, leaking from the horizontal line, drifting across the surface of the water, across the beach, falling from depths of sky. Barbara observed as he dug a hole in the sand, assembled rocks, made a fire and sat next to her on the blanket. They were eating chocolate when he suddenly remembered the cognac. He pulled a bottle that was half full from the bag and she nodded approvingly, unscrewed the cap and lifted it to her lips and took a sip, paused, drank again and handed it to him.

He swished the liquid in his mouth and swallowed and felt the warmth spread to the rest of his body. Barbara unzipped the top of her jacket, looked at Bill's profile in the glow of the fire, his well-shaped nose, slightly curved forehead, he turned his face, his patches of beard around his mouth became visible, long eyelashes, he was a very rare specimen.

"Are you cold?"

She shook her head and reached for the bottle once again.

"Does your foot still hurt?"

"It's not so bad."

He lay on the blanket and she snuggled next to him, his arm under the back of her neck, her chin against his chest. She looked at him with heavy eyes. Bill turned his face toward the dark yellow sky decorated with undulating red stripes.

"Do you think the vibration of one's soul can rediscover the frequency one had when one was born?" he heard his voice asking.

"I don't think I quite understand what you mean," she answered and yawned.

"That is, the way it was before it got distorted by all the noise we have to absorb."

She lifted her face to his.

"And imagine, if we didn't absorb all the bad things from our parents and only carried the good they gave us?" he continued, feeling her lips against his.

Barbara moved until their thighs touched. She liked Bill's hands. They were swollen from accumulated blood and brown from the sun, and lifted his hand to her cheek, then her breast and placed it on her stomach.

"What do you think Mie would say if she saw us now? You do realize she's in love with you?"

"Is she really?" Barbara asked, laughing. "Haven't you slept with her?"

"Haven't you slept with that young guy, Jonathan?"

"And what if I have?"

He shook his head, white clouds in her eyes, the foaming ocean of her mouth.

"I feel like we are two complex metal pieces that fall into place," he said.

"Mie and you?"

"No, you and me, of course."

She nodded solemnly and let her hand glide through his hair, took hold of the back of his neck and pressed his cheek against her breast and was about to ask whether the meaning of life was simply to be alive right now, but thinking it was enough.

Bill felt the heat from the bonfire, he found Barbara's hand and kissed each finger tip as his legs slid in between hers. Her body jerked.

"Did you see that?" she exclaimed.

"What?"

"A shooting star. Right in the sky above the ocean. It just went on and on."

"No, my eyes must have been closed. Did you make a wish?" Wishes raced through her like a rain of meteorites.

"I wish that..."

"Don't say it out loud or it won't happen."

"No, I wouldn't want to risk that."

She turned and felt something in him pull her and then one of his arms slid down under her back and the other across her breasts and he held tightly and she didn't want him to let go.

"A hug worth a million," Bill whispered. "My dad taught me that one."

"Can you also get one worth a billion?"

"Yes, but that's too much. Ten million, maybe. Wanna try?"

He registered her nod and slowly began to tighten his grip.

"Okay, that's expensive enough," she said in a hoarse voice.

He relaxed his arms.

"You reached six million. That's quite a lot considering it's your first try."

Bill slipped out of her embrace, fetched new branches and placed them on the bonfire. The flames lit the depression in which they were lying, the bush on top the dune stirred and he remained standing for a while letting the heat fill his body.

"My father died not far from here," Barbara suddenly said.

He sat down on the blanket and she snuggled next to him again. Then he could hear her heart beating.

"Perhaps you've heard about the accident?" she continued. "One of those little propeller planes carrying two passengers flew into a flock of seagulls and crashed and hit him. All three of them died on the spot."

Bill felt his heart stop, he mumbled that he had and wanted to say he had known the two people in the propeller plane extremely well but the words got stuck in his mouth.

"They found my father's camera, it was unharmed and in the film was a picture of a butterfly he had caught, a Real's Wood White. Do you know those?"

Bill wanted to shake his head but was unable to move. He lay on the plank bed in the hut in the wilderness and looked into the flames licking their way through the mouth of the rusty oil barrel. The wet fire wood squeaked heart-wrenchingly. In a moment he would take the ax down from the wall and plod across through the snow to the small forest area, fell a couple of thin trees, chop and place them on the bonfire so that Barbara wouldn't get cold. An all encompassing peal of thunder ripped through his brain and slowly faded. He was standing in his room behind the curtain and saw his mother looking to the house before she got into the car which backed out of the driveway, continued onto the road, it took off.

"It's just as beautiful as it is rare," said Barbara and he didn't know what she was referring to.

"The Real's Wood White," she continued. "The butterfly my father coveted the most."

Bill nodded.

"Are you tired?"

She noticed Bill's eyes wandered from star to star as though he was searching for something.

"It's strange Morten hasn't called yet, don't you think?" she asked.

"I don't understand it either." His voice sounded distant.

"What do you actually understand?" she asked, smiling as she tugged him, inhaling his scent.

"Not much," he whispered, turning his face toward her.

"Me neither."

She caught his gaze and looked into his eyes. Behind the reflection of flames from the bonfire there quivered a complexity of emotions which she recognized and which was something she hadn't seen in another human and all she wanted to do was to snuggle next to him, melt with him, and at that moment he kissed her and an overwhelming number of connections suddenly linked, new networks crisscrossing in the universe, accelerating through her body like a lightning discharge.

*

They must have fallen asleep because the day was now lying in wait behind a light blue twilight fog that encompassed the dunes and Barbara was sleeping inaudibly underneath the blanket with her back to him, the campfire softly crackling. Bill blinked his eyes when the bush at the top of the dune above him at that moment began to grow and it got skin that expanded as swelling muscles were formed. The bear looked around with his trembling snout and plodded away.

The Easiest Thing in the World

Barbara in a white bed, looked at a white-clad man who had a shiny pate, calm eyes, pressing her toes protruding from her plaster-cast foot, the cast continued up her leg and ended just below the knee.

"Good morning," it said in a speech balloon above the pate.

She was about to respond when attention was drawn to a table and chair nailed to the ceiling. On the table stood a glass with red liquid and straw.

"Two fractures, I had to put in a couple of screws, I might see you again when they have to come out. Here's to a speedy recovery."

The doctor became one with the wall. Barbara was thirsty but couldn't reach the glass. She shut her eyes hard and opened them, now the white room turned right side up except this time it was spinning like a carousel and making her nauseous.

At that moment she remembered everything. The moment something awakened her and she looked to the depression between the dunes, the crumpled blanket upon which she'd slept, the blue-gray light falling out the sky, the faintly smoldering campfire, she was thirsty, there was something she wanted to say to Bill, where was he? She caught sight of his silhouette at top of the dune, facing the ocean. Then he moved outside her scope. She sat up, her foot swollen, the skin red and tight. She got to her feet and hopped a little on one leg, crawled to the top of the dune, caught sight of the horse walking toward Bill. He placed his arms around its neck and it looked as though he was filling his body with heat from the animal that placed its head across Bill's shoulder and lowered it down his back. She managed to glide down along the dune, reestablish her balance and start hopping along. Bill turned toward her.

"Isn't this one of Morten's horses? You'd almost think it was remote controlled," she shouted and heard the echo of her own voice between the white walls.

"It's Bear."

Now she didn't know what he was referring to. And who was it standing at the open door observing her? She shut her eyes hard once again and moaned when Bill pushed her up on the horse.

He fetched the backpack and lightly patted its hind. Bear wouldn't budge, buried his muzzle against Bill's shoulder until he understood the offer included him, pulled the horse to the dune, climbed up and she felt his arms around her waist. Bear whinnied and it seemed to her a horn protruded from his forehead, wings from his sides and before any of them could react, the horse took flight toward the clouds. Her hair fluttered, time no longer existed, they had always floated there and would do so forever. The easiest thing in the world is to share your love, and she turned her head and shouted, "I think I love you, Bill."

But he didn't seem to be able to hear. The landscape of wilderness whizzed past below them, she closed her eyes, warmth from the horse's body and Bill's, the trees, the summer houses, her property lay somewhere around there, and the town, they started to descend, the main street, Morten's house, the fence. The horse stood on its four legs without a horn or wings and was grazing on dewy grass,

Bill slid off and helped her down the same way. Bear went over to the other horses. They rang the doorbell a couple times before someone opened the door, Morten's husband stood before them.

"Morten's been hospitalized," he said.

"What happened?" Barbara cried out.

"He collapsed yesterday afternoon when he was out with the horses and was picked up by a medical helicopter that flew to the nearest hospital on the mainland. They don't know what it is."

"My God," said Bill.

"Do you need medical attention?" he asked, pointing at Barbara's foot.

"It's broken, I have to get to hospital."

"You can borrow our car, I don't have a driver's license and it's not being used." He pointed toward the garage.

"Maybe you'll check in on Morten," he said shortly afterward to Bill as he handed him the car keys. "I can't go there myself because of the horses."

"Of course," said Bill.

They managed to catch the morning ferry to the mainland. Bill fetched coffee and bread and they ate in silence. The sea was calm the whole way, and they were sitting ready in the car when the ferry docked, drove along the coast toward the hospital's white buildings from a previous century that lifted themselves above the fields.

She explained to the nurse she was a doctor, they needed to take an x-ray, it was of course broken, and she was then wheeled into the operating room.

"We'll be sure to take good care of her," a voice said and she felt Bill's hand in hers, his face disappeared in the white haze of the anesthesia.

Bill sat in the chair by Barbara's bed and took her hand and she started to move. She wanted to know what he'd been doing while she was gone and he told her he'd bought coffee and found a table at the cafe, read a newspaper someone left behind and at some point she fell to sleep.

When he was sitting in the cafe he realized that he, ever since arriving to the island, hadn't given a single thought as to what was going on in the rest of the country, or world, and now he was inundated with political crises, professional commentator's observations, natural catastrophes, terror strikes, military operations, like acid, and he put the newspaper aside and went out in front of the building to smoke a cigarette. A man who, like him, smoking and sitting in a wheelchair that had a stand with a bag connected to it filled with yellow liquid that entered his body via his hand, told about diabetes and other ailments he suffered and Bill listened until he suddenly remembered Morten, put out the cigarette and managed to say "Hope you get well soon" on his way to the glass gates.

The man sitting in the reception informed him

where he could find Morten but visiting hours wouldn't start for a couple of hours, so he went back to the cafe, bought a weekly journal and dozed in the company of the rich and royal.

Barbara budged and her eyes opened and she smiled, nodded toward the glass with red juice and he lifted the straw to her lips.

"Morten's on the floor above," he said.

It took her a few seconds to process the information before she nodded.

"Have you seen him?" she asked in a whisper, cleared her throat. Her eyes beginning to come to life.

He shook his head, felt her pulling his hand and he leaned over and she continued to pull until he kissed her lips, a little dry, and her mouth turned into a smile and he kissed her again and let his other hand rest on her back.

"I think I love you, too" he whispered in her ear which apparently tickled because she shook her head.

*

Bill found a wheel chair in the hallway and helped Barbara into it and they rolled to the elevator and took it up one flight, stopped in front of a door, listened for sounds within. Bill knocked and rolled in. A tanned face protruded from all the whiteness, a leg, an arm. Morten opened his eyes.

"I'll say."

"We didn't mean to disturb you."

"What are you doing here? What happened, Barbara?"

"I managed to break my foot but your husband said..."

"It could be anything, they're looking into it, I was gone and then came back. I've come to realize I am my body."

He activated the electric bed so he was sitting up.

"How did you manage to break your foot? It's not exactly easy to do." He pointed to the cast.

"I fell on the beach."

"How unfortunate." He looked up.

"But Bill, what brings you here?"

"I drove Barbara to the operation. In your car, by the way."

Morten's slender fingers slid through his gray curls and he nodded thoughtfully. At that moment there was a knock at the door and someone opened it. Jonathan entered and stopped abruptly, Morten started.

"Quite a turnout here," Jonathan exclaimed, looking from one to the other. Whereupon he quickly went over to the bed.

"What happened, Dad?"

He wrapped his arms around his frail body, kissed his cheeks and sat at the edge of the bed and tears welled up in Morten's eyes.

"This is my son, Jonathan," he said.

"Mom's dead," Jonathan said in a subdued voice and slid into his father's arms and continued to hold on to him.

Morten made a long sigh.

"It's a good thing she got hospitalized," Morten said in a coarse voice. "But I didn't expect for it to go this fast."

Jonathan sat up.

"I shut off the respirator," he said out to the room, shaking his head imperceptibly.

"It couldn't go on. Now she's on her way to the world beyond, if you believe in that sort of thing."

Jonathan looked at Bill, who nodded and it dawned on him cause and effect were one and the same and his gaze slid out the window just when the clouds at that very moment opened for the sun and a yellow light grazed across the fields.

Jonathan pointed at Barbara's leg with concern.

"It's no big deal, the foot will grow again," she said.

Jonathan turned to his father.

"Don't worry, kid, you won't be orphaned just yet," Morten said, smiling tiredly.

"Do you promise?"

"I'll be out of here in no time, just you wait and see."

"Should we perhaps say our goodbyes now, we'll all see each other back on the island?" Bill asked, taking hold of the wheel chair.

They looked at him in silence.

"Get better soon, Morten," said Barbara. "I didn't know you were father and son."

"We haven't seen much of one another in recent years," Morten said, taking hold of Jonathan's hand and placing it on his chest. "There have been so many things."

Bill grabbed hold of the door handle.

"Barbara, would you stand in for me until I'm back on track?" Morten asked.

She started laughing.

"Of course."

The Sun Behind the Sun

Barbara was permitted to go home, equipped with crutches. Bill helped her get settled into the car and they drove along the water and she sensed a cloud-soft calm settle around her, made do with nodding, shaking her head when he asked if she was okay, exhausted, and when they turned in at the harbor the ferry lay in wait, she placed her hand on his thigh and he lifted it to his mouth and kissed it.

They found a bench on the deck, she swung her plaster cast up on it. Out on the ocean the wind came, the ferry rocked lightly back and forth, the collar of Barbra's jacket fluttered and the gold heart her ex-husband had given her when he proposed to her hit her face, she put it back under her shirt, zipped up and felt Bill's arm around her hip. He pulled her close and said he had been reproaching himself for that which he hadn't had the courage to do.

He looked at her. "But it's never too late to change direction."

"Is that what you are in the course of doing?" she asked.

He nodded.

"You've been used to thinking one way and now you're being forced to think another. What are your plans?"

He didn't know how to answer her.

After the death of my father I was told he owned a piece of property here on this island. I have kept it," she said after a few seconds hesitation.

Bill looked at her.

"I want to show it to you. My father's plan was to build a house. The drawings from back then still exist."

The movements of the ferry made him feel dizzy but he didn't let it show.

"My little brother is a carpenter and he builds wooden houses for a living. I'm just sayin'," he said.

Barbara scrutinized him.

"I sometimes try to imagine what his final minutes were like. Perhaps he was sitting on a stool in the little black shed in the middle of the property in the meadow between the pine trees. There was one, and it was what the plane hit when it crashed.

Maybe he was daydreaming about the house he wanted to build. It had to be red and have windows with small panes, an open plan kitchen and living room, three rooms, a sauna, a wood-fired hot tub."

Bill's mind began to stir. He had to tell her the truth, and it had to be now.

"Barbara, there's something I have to tell you."

"At some point the sound of a humming engine must have reached my father's ears," she continued as though she hadn't heard him, "but he probably didn't register it since the airport was very close by."

He hesitated, looked at the sky, suddenly she smiled broadly.

"I bet he had a lunch pack with him. So he'd taken his lunch out of the bag and I know exactly what it consisted of: two pieces of home-made sourdough bread with country ham, cream cheese with caraway seeds, and green pepper. As he was eating he was probably looking across the sea through a window covered in spider webs."

"So the property has a view of the sea?"

"Yes, it's very well situated. I think he was sitting and observing the foam of the wave crests, he could also hear wind in the trees, perhaps a cone hit the felted roof and he looked up and concluded what it was and shortly after wondered what the screeching sound was that continued to grow louder and louder and then..."

"He and my parents died," said Bill.

Barbara turned to him. He couldn't read the expression on her face.

"You already knew?" he asked.

Her telephone vibrated in her jacket pocket. Bill saw it was Jonathan and got up. She looked at him and nodded and he didn't know what her nod referred to. She covered the phone with her hand and took a hold of his arm.

"I know now," she said and her eyes penetrated his and she pulled him to her and they held each other before she gently pushed him away and placed the phone to her ear.

When Bill crossed the deck toward the railing his mind was empty and he registered how his feet let go of the foundation underneath them and his body lifted itself a centimeter, two, three, across the deck, the tension in the back of his neck, in his entire body disappeared, he leaned forward, received the caress of wind and let his gaze disappear in the waves.

"A moment ago the sky exploded in a brilliant light across the fields surrounding this hospital."

Jonathan's voice in her ear, she was shaking within, looking at Bill who was standing at the railing and looking in toward the mainland.

"I can discern Sirius out there behind the sun. Do you see Sirius?" Jonathan continued.

"I think so."

She looked across the water and let her gaze graze the sun.

"Do you also see the glowing thread that connects everything together?"

"Yes, I do."

"The earth does not belong to us, we belong to the earth, the universe, we are at one with the force from which all life derives and perishes. ... are you there, Barbara?"

"Jonathan?"

"The birds sing of my longing. When the forest turns yellow we'll be together again and the joy of it melts my heart."

Bill turned around just at the very same moment the sun broke through clouds and hit Barbara's face. She was no longer talking on the telephone.

The ferry was approaching the harbor and he went

back and helped her to her feet. They moved across deck, stopped in front of the door to the lounge. She turned, the shadows of clouds drifted like abandoned ships on the surface of the water. Bill held the door, quickly kissed her as she passed and she stopped and pulled him toward her and heard him breathing deeply. Then he took a step forward and shut the door behind them.

THANK YOU

Thank you to Poul Vedelsby (1939-2008) for the world's biggest and most affectionate hug.

Thank you to Karen Mathilde Gielstrup (1912-2011) for all your love.

Thank you to Bjørn Felsager (1949-2015) for your compassion and wisdom – and for the title of this book.

Thank you to Niels Birger Wamberg (1930-2020) for your friendship through four decades.

*

And thank you to Rane Willerslev for many consciousness-expanding travels and discussions.

Nina Sokol is a poet in the midst of translating novels, short stories. plays and poems by Danish writers. She was a grant poet-in-residence at The Vermont Studio Center in 2011 and has received several grants from the Danish Art's Council to translate plays, including a play written by the fairy tale writer H.C. Andersen which was published by the journal InTranslation. Her own poems have appeared in American journals, including Miller's Pond and the Hiram Poetry Review and a collection is now available from Spuyten Duyvil, *The Silence Sound Makes*.

JAKOB VEDELSBY's seven novels speak to an international audience. An eighth novel will be published in Denmark in 2025 where his first poetry will also see publication. Vedelsby has received extensive recognition as well as awards from the Danish Arts Foundation, among others. He holds an M.A. in Film and Media Studies and between 2014 and 2017 served as chair of the Danish Society of Authors. He resides in Copenhagen.